Finding a Light in the Darkness of War:

The Return of Merlin

Book 2

By: A. P. Whitfield

Dedication

To those who still believe in magick and a better place. To my fellow witches, I love you all. Keep being beautiful and amazing.

Blessed Be

Chapter 1

October 20, 2021

     "Things have not been the same since last October when Merlin went missing, hell… when we all learned that Daniel was Merlin, and that Merlin was actually real. This is just more to add to the crazy events. If only this was a story about a girl living a normal life and has a normal job and a normal boyfriend and does everything like normal people…. but I don't. In fact, I am sitting in my car driving to my old high school… well not Prospero but the other school I got moved to when all hell broke loose at Prospero but anyways where was I? Oh yes, driving to do student teaching hoping that I don't run into my ex-boyfriend who is my old English teacher. Sadly, that isn't even what makes me abnormal from everyone else. If you're wondering yes, I am talking to myself in my car listening to *A Thousand Miles by Vanessa Carlton* narrating my life into a tape recorder like I am some sappy 90's early 2000 movie." I sigh to myself, "I really need a life." I pull into the school at Salem High School and find a parking spot. "Okay, let's get this over with. It's lunch so I should have time to find the room number I am looking for since they redid the school." I get out and grab my bag looking around making sure I have everything I needed before I locked my door and went in and over to the office to check in and get my guest pass and the paper showing where I go. Wondering around the school looking at the new building I get grabbed and pulled into a room. Thinking to myself when I see who it is who grabbed me so roughly, *'ah shit. Just my luck.'*

     "What are you doing here?" He asked as he had me push against the

wall his fierce eyes on me. I could smell his after shave with how close he was, so I knew he had to be able to smell the perfume I had that was my favorite, "I asked you a question. What are you doing back here?"

I knew we didn't have long before the bell would ring for classes to change, and other teachers would be in and out of the teacher's lounge. I spoke soft and calm to him, "I am here to do an observational check list for one of my classes back at school. I have a note of approval because this is a grade. Now do let me go. I did not come for you. We're through. You made that rather clear."

I felt the gap between us closing in and him taking in my scent. He quickly pulled away from me as a teacher came in with a coffee cup looking for a refill. I recognized her quickly as an old teacher of mine. She looked between him and I noticing some obvious tension.

"Stella I will be back do not move." He went into the teacher's lounge restroom and left me, and my past teacher Mrs. Fits a lone.

"So, care to tell what is going on here?" Any other time I could have been honest with her but not now with things between James Kirkwood and me.

"No, it's nothing Mrs. Fits. I really should get back to my project the whole reason why I am here." I say to her.

"Hum he may not be too happy to see you gone when he comes out." Mrs. Fits looked me over with a knowing look at this point but did not comment on it.

I looked at the door, "if he really needs to talk to me, he will find me but for now I must go," I picked up my notebook and my small rucksack with my initial on it. I didn't look back as I quickly left the room trying to put as much distance between him and I so I could think and get my thoughts together. Turning a corner, I found the girls restroom and I felt a sigh of a relief as I went in and found a stall to lock myself in.

Thinking to myself, '*Stella what are you doing? Why didn't you stay back to talk to him? Wait why does he want to talk anyways he's the one who ghosted you and even deleted you off Facebook. Whatever. Just stay in control of your emotions or your magick will do something on its own free will again. The last time you lost control you had to play it off like a freak storm must have blown through. That is if you ever see him again. I really need to stop narrating my life like this.*' Slapping my forehead at how ridiculous I was being.

As my mind overflowed with thoughts, I heard giggling girls come in the

restroom realizing it was class change. I open my stall door and walk to the sink to wash my hands. I look at my reflection just as the other girls did. We stood refreshing our makeup and lipstick then took a moment to fix our hair. I pulled out my brush and brushed my long deep red hair. My bright green eyes looking back at me more confident and readier this time if he decided to look for me.

The bell rang as I left the restroom and students quickly get into classrooms. I found the room letter and number D13 the office gave me to the new door of the class I could sit in on. Knocking on the door only to find Mr. Kirkwood on the other side *'well fuck,'* I thought, *'just my damn luck,'* I look at him his eyes still a fierce green and his dark hair tousled falling slightly in his face. Feeling a build of confidence, I smile a seductive smile and bat my eyelashes at him as I hand him the note from the office. He took it reading it over before allowing me in.
He presented me to the class as he leaned on his desk with his arms crossed over his blue button down that I quickly recognized. Smiling at the memories and pushing it out of my mind for the time being.
"Class this is Estella you may call her Stella if she is okay with that. She is here visiting from a university for a project she must do. I ask you all to be on your best behavior because I will grade you for this. Now if you will open The Crucible as I pass the books out, we will be reading it this week."

I walked to his desk sitting my bag down behind it and ready my notebook and pen to take notes on the class when I hear him say what they would be reading. Remembering that we read it and I played the part of Abigail and him John Proctor.
"Stella," snaps me out of my daze, "will you help take part in reading the lines with us? You did such a splendid job when you took part back when you were in high school." He studied me for a moment with amusement in his eyes.
"I guess I can. May I ask which part I will be reading?" Handing me a book feeling the class watching every move we make as I open to the first page.
"Would you do Abigail again?" James asked me while he finished passing out the rest of the books to his last period class.
"Sure, why not." I respond knowing good and well what his next words was going to be with who he would be acting out.
"Great! I will be John Proctor." He clapped his hands together and walked back over to his desk to grab his copy of the book.

'*Go figure.*' I said to myself.

"Now to give the class their parts and we will get started." James looked over the class and started to place each student with their assigned parts. As he gave out the parts I watched the class and how they behaved taking mental notes for my notebook.

"Hey," a voice next to me whisper and I give him a side glance as I notice him checking me out licking his lips like he was ready to pounce, "how about I take you out for a good time?"

I turn and look at him and cross my arms over my chest as I see him checking out my legs wishing I hadn't worn a dress now. I was self-conscious over my appearance. I was by no means a slender girl. I was considered curvy or somewhat thick. Pushing aside my own negative thoughts I managed to reply.

"One stop checking me out, two you and I will never happen, three I don't date teenagers and four you're not my type." I feel James come up behind me.

"What is going on here." I turn to look at him only to see he was giving his student a hard stare down.

"Nothing Mr. Kirkwood just trying to ask her out..." The young male replied in confusion over the glare he was getting from James.

"She is off limits, and I will hear no more about it." James retorts hotly.

I let out a long staggering breath as I catch his eye aware now the whole class went silent watching us.

The student looked between us and smirked, "why are you calling dibs on her?"

As soon as those words left that kids mouth James had him jerked up from his desk and out the door. I felt my face turning red and all eyes on me as I stood alone in front of the class.

"So...is that kid always like that?" I chuckled nervously playing with the book in my hands.

"Pretty much. He thinks he's hot shit and can get away with anything because his dad owns a country club and is a lawyer. My name is Raven by the way." One girl spoke sounding like she's told this story before.

"Well, that is just lovely… I guess while they're doing that maybe I can learn everyone else's names. We will start with you." I point to a shy girl wearing glasses.

In nothing but a whisper, "Lidia."

Then it went down the rows each one saying who they were. Taking notes to

remember each of them. Twelve kids in all including Gabriel who went to the office.

"Well, there is a good number of you six boys and six girls."
The bell rang and that was the end of the day everyone gathered their things making their way out the door. I was ready to do the same when James made his way back in and over to me. Before he spoke, he made sure we were alone.
"We need to talk and how I approached you earlier that wasn't the way to do it and I apologize." He ran his fingers through his dark hair as he spoke.
"Okay apology accepted now what do you want to talk about?"
I sat my stuff down and took a seat on a desk while he started pacing the front of the classroom gathering his thoughts.
He stopped back in front of me, "Stella. We never talked about what happened between us and I know that is my fault."

"Yes, it is, but go on." I crossed my arms over my chest waiting for him to continue.
"Um...yes well," nervousness in his voice as he went on, "what we were doing...it wasn't right I was worried about losing my job even though you were graduated but I was still worried about what everyone would say. I know it was like I lead you on with talks of whisking you away too far off places, but I really do care about you, and I know that wasn't the end of our story even when I cut you out of my life..."

"Stop! Just stop! You couldn't have thought of all of that before we had sex? Before I gave myself to you, you were my first. Not just once but multiple times. Plus let's not fool ourselves we were bored remember. It wasn't meant to get serious even though it was. I got tired of just being a secret and all the private meetings and red wine kisses under the sheets. I wanted to be more than that. Then out of the blue you ghosted me!" I could feel my anger building up inside of me as my anxiety kicked in.
"I'm sorry, okay? I let my job and ego get in the way of it all, but it didn't mean nothing to me it meant something..." He replied quickly.
Silence fell in his classroom as we looked at each other with memories flashing back and the tension between us growing. Before one of us could say another word, a voice came over the intercom in his room.
"Mr. Kirkwood; Gabriel's mother is here and wishes to speak with you are you free?"

"Yes, send her to my room." He said flatly to the voice over the intercom.
"Okay, she is on her way."
The intercom cuts out then silence sets in again.
"I guess I need to go." I gather my things again to leave.
"Can I see you tonight?" He takes my arm to turn me around to face him.
I thought a moment and let out a sigh. "Yes, here is my address to my condo
I will be home all-night studying." I gave him the paper when I finished and
walked to the door as a woman came in and looked at my necklace. An
amethyst and rose quartz magically fused together. She looked into my eyes
and took my hand to act as if she was introducing herself. I felt such a shock
of power from her but kept a straight face just as she did, and I knew she
knew what I was. Much like I knew what she was now. She wore no crystal
like I did but I felt her power as she shook my hand.
"Hello, I am Cathy Calaway and you are?" She introduced herself to me
with a fake smile spread over her face.
"Stella." I pulled my hand away getting the feeling I couldn't trust her.
"Stella was just leaving she was here to do a project and I am afraid Gabriel
prevented much of that." James walked over to us to invite Mrs. Calaway
into his classroom to be able to sit and talk with her.

Chapter 2

I slipped out of his room and felt my necklace on me was warm to the touch.

'No wonder Gabriel thinks he can do what he wants his mom is a witch so he must be a witch as well,' I thought to myself as I walked to my car.

It took me ten to fifteen minutes to get home. I decided not to do my homework; instead, I opened a bottle of Ecco Domino Chardonnay and started myself a hot bubble bath. Thinking out loud, "okay....so James is coming over to pick up where we left of on our arguing plus he has a witch in his class. Mom is a witch...so is dad a witch also or just your everyday average Joe." Soaking in the tub drinking wine I let my mind wonder as Ludwig van Beethoven played in the background. Thirty minutes passed when I looked at the clock.

"Well, I need to get out he will be over at some point. To cook or not to cook... Eh I'm ordering pizza." I let out the bath water and put on gray Victoria Secrets lounging pants and T-shirt then order a large veggie pizza with extra black olives from Dominoes.

"I think I may call Stevie and see what she thinks of the Calaways." Picking up my phone after just sitting it down I press the name and called her. It rings a few times before she picks up and I tell her everything. "So.... what do you think?"

"Were you wearing anything that could have told her you were a witch?" She questioned as she hushed a voice I could hear in the background.

"Is that Stella? Can I talk to her? Let me talk to her." The voice sounded.

"Chester. Hush. Chester says hey." Stevie chuckled into the phone as an obvious pout could be heard over the phone.

"Yes...my crystals but that shouldn't be a big give away." I giggled, "hello

14

Chester. I will see you both very soon."

"That is true." Stevie giggled in return then let out a sigh. "She must have wanted to make contact with you to be sure otherwise you could of look like an average flower child that meditates. You know crystals are becoming all the rage now." She teased.

We both laugh at that, and I hear a knock at the door. I hang up with Stevie to answer the door finding James on the other side holding the pizza and seeing the Dominoes guy pull out.

"Um I needed to tip him." I said looking slightly confused.

"Don't worry I got it." He steps in and goes to sit the pizza down.

"Yeah come in. Make yourself at home." I said sarcastically.

He laughs and sits down at the small table in the kitchen.

"Do you want some wine?" I let out a sigh and close my door.

"Sure...nice little place you have here." He let his eyes wonder around the space.

I get down another wine glass and pour him a glass then join him at the table. "Thank you...so why did you feel the need to see me tonight?"

He sipped his wine then looked in the glass as if he was searching for answers, but none came so we sat quietly till he finally spoke. "When I saw you today it brought back memories of us and how stupid I was for giving you up. I don't know what I thought I could do by coming here tonight...I guess I thought I could win you back...."

Again, silence fell over the room.

"James....I am not going to run back to you for it to go back to how it was. I will not become secret on the side again." I broke the silence that was becoming defining.

"Yes, I know....it won't be like that I promise." His voice sounded broken and sad as he spoke.

I look down at my glass of wine not sure if I could believe him or not when I felt my necklace go warm on my chest then sensing danger was coming.

"Shit..." Ever since what happened last year it became important that a lot of the witches charm their crystals of choice to warm up at the sense of danger.

"What?" James asked catching the tone of my voice and my expression on my face.

"I don't have time to explain but come with me." I get up and go to my room and quickly change into black running pants, sports bra and a baggy black tank top then put on my running shoes and grab a rucksack in the

corner by the door.

"What is going on?" He asked with confusion in his voice.

"Do you believe in witches James?" I asked him quickly.

"What? No!" He looked at me like I was crazy.

"Well start believing. I am one and some very bad ones are closing in, so we don't have long. Stay close to me." I explained as I got everything ready to go.

"Have you lost your damn mind?" He questions.

I roll my eyes, "fine I'll prove it." I snap my fingers and fire danced in the palm of my hand and then I made it vanish as fast as it appeared, "do you believe me now? Let's go!"

Before he could snap out of being shocked, I had us out the door and to my car. My necklace grew hotter and almost at a glow as they got closer. "Dammit they're moving fast. Get in the car now!" His eyes wide and without a word got into my car. I cranked my car and backed out fast then put it in drive. Feeling my necklace slowly cool down as I put as much distance between them and us. I look over and he still looked shocked and confused. "I guess the cat is out of the bag now. Do you have any questions?"

"How long have you been a witch?" He asked breathlessly

"All my life but our magick doesn't come in fully till we are eight. That is when we take a test to get placed in the schools of our parents choosing. They are schools of magick. I was in Prospero School of Magick before I was taken out and sent to the school you teach at. Along with other students that was pulled out… there is a war going on in the realm of magick that is the cause of it. A lot of magick based families think in doing this it will help save them and their kids… at first it was just to protect them at what was going on at the school… it was only happening at Prospero, but it quickly started to happen at all the schools of magick. Students and families being attacked… now a lot of bad is happening… Merlin… he is… was real… or is… he risked his life saving us…. There is a group trying to find him again… because now things are getting worse."

"So, Merlin is real, and a war is going on? Where are we going?" He tried to take in everything at once that I told him. I knew it was a lot to take in. Hell, I was still trying to understand how thing had gotten this bad.

"Well, I am not fully sure who is after me...well now us but I have an idea. The Calaways. Oh, and we're going to Stevie's she is a witch as well."

"So…. Gabriel and his parents are the bad guys and top of that you and Stevie are witches?"
He lays his head back and rubs his temple as if to fight off a headache. I smile over at him and turn into Stevie's driveway.

"Well, we're here. Come on we don't have time to play around we can do that after we find out what the Calaways' are up to." I grab my bag as we get out of the car and head up to the walkway to her front door. Before I even rang the doorbell, she was answering the door.
"Hurry come in Chester just left. I thought I felt you here and…" She stops short when she sees James, "well hello Mr. Kirkwood."
"Stevie it is always good to see you." He comes in behind me.

"You left out the part of him paying you a visit when we were on the phone earlier." She whispered loudly as she closes the door and leads us to the living room. "Take a seat." She nods to the couch.
"Well, I wasn't sure he really was coming over or not." I laughed a slight embarrassed laugh and poked both my index fingers together.
"I'm going out on a limb here and guessing you told Stevie about us?" He asked taking a set next to me.
"Yes, I did I tell her everything. Where are your parents, Stevie?" I looked around the large room that I had spent a lot of time in with Stevie.
"At a gathering. Where we're about to go but first we need to get you guys changed for it." She gave a little grin at the remark.
"Why what's wrong with what we have on?" James asked clearly confused.
"This isn't a normal gathering it is a cult of witches that are meeting to discuss the breakouts of attacks from the enemy cult that want to break the balance of the magick world and nonmagical world. The enemy thinks the nonmagical should bow down to us and don't believe in hiding their magick from those that do not have powers whereas our cult believes in living in peace with them and only using our powers for good." Stevie states in a matter-of-fact kind of way.

"Then we need to get there and find out just what part the Calaways play in it. Only thing I wonder is, I did not feel anything from Gabriel my necklace didn't react to him like it did his mom or an hour ago."
"That is strange." Stevie rubbed her chin and made a face of concentration as she turned on her heels to go to the stairs that lead up to the sleeping quarters.

"Has it always been able to pick up on magick kind?" James said looking at my necklace.

"Not always. It can manly feel witches and warlock but siren, mermaids, fairies or changelings and even demons and sorcerers it can't detect that well. There are talismans that can search them out I have a few but have never had the need to use them. We're not at war with any of them even if the enemy does try to get them join their side."

"Well, I am worried the demons and changelings will want to join them they're getting restless." Stevie says worried as she leads us upstairs to change clothes, "James you can borrow some of my brother's clothes." She stops at the first bedroom and hunts in her brother's closet for a long black cloak with a hood. "Here just put this black shirt on and this cloak your dress pants are fine they're black just keep your head low when we go, and you will kinda blind in. Okay Stella your turn, off to my room."

We leave him to change to go find me something to wear. In her room down the hall, I sit on her bed as she opens an old trunk and takes out two Victorian dresses a deep purple one for her with a corset a lot like the other in dark green one for me. We help each other into the dresses and tighten the corset back. I look in the full-length mirror noticing the incredible detail of the dresses with ribbon crisscrossing the front of the bodice with a swooping collar showing off some cleavage and it tightens through the torso and full at the waist down.

"Wow..." My mouth dropped at the sight. I had not worn one of these dresses in a while and I always loved how they made me look and feel when I slipped them on.

"I know right? I love getting to wear these. Here is a cloak and boots." She handed me the last of the outfit and I sat down to lace up the black combat boots and put on the black cloak. Stevie was a beautiful girl with raven black hair and gray eyes. She was fair complected like I was only she did not have the freckles that I had. We were built about the same only she was an inch shorter being 5'1 and me being 5'2 and her slightly thicker but not by much.

"Well, I think we're ready." I say standing up taking one last look at myself feeling more like a witch now than ever before. I look at her and smile, "I think this is selfie worthy."

She laughs with me and pulls out her phone for us to take a picture.

"I'm sending it to your phone now." She pulled up my name and sent it to me with my phone going off as it receives the picture text. I pull it up and looked at it smiling brightly. "Yeah. I know. We are babes."

"Thank you my dear and I have to agree now let's go." We come out of her room to see James ready and waiting for us.

He looks up to see us; his eyes widen taking in our appearance, "wow...you look bewitching."

I smile at his choice of words remembering he always knew how to say the right thing and that made him that much more charming. "So where are we going to be dressed up like this?" He asked making a wide gesture of our now wardrobe change.

With a smile, "to a graveyard of course."

"I should have known anytime I am with you we end up at a graveyard. That should have been my first hint that something was off about you but who would have known it was the fact you're a witch." Smiling he shakes his head making his dark hair fall in front of his beautiful green eyes. I reach out and slightly move his hair from his eyes caught in each other's stares.

"Um....so yeah if you two are done making googly eyes at each other we should really go."

We both blush and follow Stevie back down the steps and I grab my bag as we head out the door to her small SUV.

Chapter 3

Getting in her vehicle, "I need to pick up Chester before we head to the gathering."

"Okay sounds good." I get in the back seat instead with James leaving the seat open for Chester later.

Driving a few blocks away to his condo Stevie pulls into his complex that he moved to for college, "I'll be right back."

She gets out and leaves the SUV running and what used to be our song comes on the radio; *Carousel by Sam Tsui.* We let the lyrics play out before one of us says or does anything. He takes my hand in his and brings it to his lips kissing my finger lightly. My breathing becomes shaky as flashbacks of us play out in my mind. I look over at him and we held each other's eyes as he pulls me to him closing the gap between us.

My heart starts beating fast recognizing this feeling all too well.

"James...." Taking my breath away his lips find mine; he takes and holds the back of my head as I get engulfed in his kisses and forget how to breath.

Hearing the car doors open we pull away from each other reluctantly only for me to lay my head on his chest hearing his heart beating just as fast as mine. Stevie looks at us with amusement. "Chester, you know Stella, and this is Stella's ex-boyfriend James."

Chester puts his hand out and shakes James's hand giving him a suspicious look, "nice to meet you, James. Now can we go get food?"

"No, we do not have time. How are you always hungry I will never know?" Stevie rolled her eyes in response to seeing Chester cross his arms over his chest and pouts.

James taking his hand back giving Chester a hard look. We drove in silence to the gathering, and I look out of the window into the night still wondering what was with those looks the guys gave each other. Thinking that Stevie had told Chester about James and our relationship and how he broke my heart before I just assume, he doesn't trust him that James won't do it again. Leaving it at that thought we turn off on a dirt road; we drive a few miles through wooded area and arrive in a clearing where several other vehicles where parked and seeing others getting out walking to the pavilion in the middle of the graveyard.

As we're walking, we see other witches dancing to music by the river that leads to a big lake.
Most dancing naked by the moonlight at the river edge with each other, their long hair hardly covering their breast as they danced with each other. It was an enchanting sight to watch at how free they were dancing in the light of the full moon.

"What are they doing?" James whispered to me.
"They're dancing for the moon Hunter's Moon." I smiled at the women.
"But why?" asking another question clearly confused why anyone would dance for a moon.
"Good question," we kept walking to the meeting point, "they're doing it to thank the sun and moon for a bountiful harvest. I would say they have been out here all day and night dancing and making love with their partners or each other. I guess you could say they are the hippies of the witches." He didn't say anything after that I guess he was just taking my word for it. Reaching the center, the leader began to start the meeting.

"Fellow witches it burdens me to say this, but our enemy clan tried to use their magick openly today and not only that, but we have a traitor in a fellow clan from the siren. We do not know who it is or the reason for it, but we do know from the witches we captured today the head warlock of that clan has recruited a siren and that is all we were told for now. We are working on getting more information from them."
As he went on Stevie whispered to me, "this isn't good once one group joins them then we really will be divided. I know it is only one person with them now, but it only takes one person to bring more in to join them."
"I know...but we mustn't think that way. Let's just pray whoever joined them only plans to use that insight they gain against them. If that could be true it would help us a great deal to bring down the enemy." I took her hand in mine and gave it a gentle squeeze for comfort.
"I hope you're right Stella...that person would be brave to go in alone to do that." She held onto my hand a little longer to calm herself.

"Me too. I need to call Victoria and see what she makes of all of this. We also need to see Sebastian." I played with her fingers out of habit to work to calm my own nerves.

"Want to see Sebastian?" She looked at me with amusement and an arched brow.

"Yes, he can help us." I looked at her with confusion at her expression.

"So, you want to take your non magical lover to see your magical lover to get a card reading?" Stevie teased.

"Well, when you put it that way it sounds bad." I respond with a scowl. She smiles at me, and we both hold back laughter. The leader finishes talking, and everyone brakes into small groups talking in worried voices. It was something to be worried about the magick realm has been thrown into chaos.

The guys approached us from where they had stopped and listened to the speech.

"What now?" Chester asked when he got close.

"Now we go home change clothes and get rest for tomorrow because that is when planning starts." Stevie replied looking at us three; her raven black hair fitting her beautiful sharp facial features showing off in the moon light. Her gray eyes serious as she studied our faces taking her next words with serious thought, "none of this is safe we may not even live if we get caught and so many are involved and some from our clan has died already.... we could be next. We have to be careful who we trust."

Those words hung over us as we stood silently only noise, I could hear was the giggling of the dancing witches in the background wishing I could break free like that and feel free spirited this time like I did last year. Cold chills from those words she spoke made me shiver as a light fall breeze blew our cloaks around us. I pulled mine more around me.

"Well, I guess first things first. James, we need to take you to pack a suitcase and pack a couple of weeks' worth and anything else you will need. You're involved now and I would say they will come looking for you. Next, we will go back to my place, and I will do the same and see if anyone has been there and left clues." I spoke seeing a plan fold out in my head, "guys this is going to be a wild ride."

"Well, us standin around isn't getting our plans in gear so let's move out and get this freak show on the road." Chester said with a smirk on his face running his hand through his shaggy brown hair, his Scottish accent thick as it rolled off his tongue.

"I will call Victoria in the car and see if the fairies have said anything." I speak. Victoria had gone to another school. We did not become friends until we both were sent to Salem High School and met.

"Wait Victoria? Victoria Bradly is a fairy? Is there any of you I taught that isn't magical of some kind?" James looked at Stevie and I in shock.

Stevie and I started laughing at his question as we got in her car and headed back into town.

"Yes, plenty are that you taught. Mostly the ones we hung out with are of the magick realm, so it was very few. A lot either go off to private magick school or are home schooled." I told him as we drove down the gravel path away from the gathering. I looked over at him noticing that he was trying to remember who I hung around with. We get to his house thirty minutes later and Chester goes in and helps him pack then we go back to my condo and as expected it had been trashed in attempt in looking for all my magical objects that I kept in one bag. Stevie helps me pack clothes and anything else I needed plus the pizza, then we were out the door and back on the road to her house.

We were all lost in thought taking in the events that had happened today the feeling of stress and nervousness overflow my mind making my hands cold and feeling sick to my stomach. When we got back to her house, I was ready for bed and to put this day behind me. Grabbing our bags and pizza we go in, and Stevie shows James to one of the guest rooms and Chester found his.

"Stevie, do you care if I go on to your room and get ready for bed?" I asked her ready to get out of the dress wondering why I even though the thing was great in the first place as the corset cut off my breathing. Now I understood why Elizabeth from that one pirate movie passed out into the water.

"Yeah, go ahead I am going to get the guys set up and I will be in to help with the gown if you need it." Stevie looked back at me and gave me a warm smile.

"I think I got it if not I will let you know." I headed off down the hall with an uneasy feeling with all that happened today. I found her room that we've had plenty of sleep overs in and remembering all that we used to do growing up from playing with dolls to painting each other's nails and talking about boys. It is crazy to think that those innocent childhood days have gone by so fast and even going into high school still ignorant to how the outside world really was and once being those free-spirited witches that

danced naked by the moon light. Still thinking about those times as I undo the corset and stepping out of the dress, I put it neatly back in the trunk and put my lounging clothes on. I hear whispering in the hallway next to Stevie's door sounding serious and hushed as I listened gathering my things to wash my face.

"Chester are you sure?" I heard Stevie say.

"Yes, I don't think we can trust James I keep getting bad feelings from him. I could be wrong, but we just cannot let our guard down around him." Chester retorts as he whispered to her.

"Chester if I tell Stella this it will kill her." They go quiet both thinking about what was just said,

"I hate to say it, but I have been getting these same feelings about him. Something isn't right about him...something I have never felt from him before. I think it is best to keep this between us and to keep a close watch on him in case he does try something." Stevie sounded as if she held worry in her voice. I had not noticed anything different from James but then again, I guess I was blinded from my feelings I held for him.

"I agree. I will take the guest room across from his so I can keep watch on him." I hear them kiss goodnight and I dash for the bathroom and start removing my makeup trying to act like I didn't just hear more heart-breaking news to stress me out more. Stevie knocks on the bathroom door before coming in to get ready for bed.

"You know you don't have to knock you've seen me pee out in a field before and same for me." We both laugh and she splashes me with the sink water and before long we were both drenched in water and laughing so hard, we were crying. We hear a knock at the bedroom door and yell for them to come in. It was Stevie's parents and the amusement on their faces when they saw the bathroom and us was priceless.

"Are we interrupting something?" Stevie's dad asked. Luke was a tall man with broad shoulders and a strong built. You would have thought he was a warrior rather than a witch. He wore his dark hair back in a short ponytail showing off his strong jaw line and his chocolate brown eyes. His suit fitting perfectly and Stevie's mom in a dress like the ones we wore but looked far more elegant and filed it out more in the bust than we did. Her long golden hair hung down her back and her bright crystal blue eyes shining at us as she giggled and hugged us both.

"Oh, hey Luke and Phoebe we were just getting ready for bed." I greeted them both with a warm smile as I dried my face and arms off with a little

hand towel.

"Really is that why you both are drenched to the bones and laughing so loud we heard you in the kitchen." Said Phoebe with a smile as she got us towels to dry off, "it is good to see you again Stella. How was school this week? I know you and Stevie have been getting ready for finals. Oh, and James seems lovely are you both back together or are you still with Sebastian?"

"Mom! Privacy much?" Stevie took the towel and patted down herself and her wet clothes.

"I am just asking." Phoebe held up her hands in defense.

I laugh and blush, "no it's okay I'm still with Sebastian, James and I are just friends but really I am not serious about either right now because of school. I am more focused on graduating next year."

"Oh well good for you that is a very smart way to think. Well, we're off to bed don't have too much fun you two." Her parents left the room and we changed out of our wet clothes into some dry ones.

"Okay go on I know you want to ask I saw that side glance you gave me when your mom asked about James." I pulled my red hair up into a messy bun and walked into her bedroom to sit down and eat the pizza I had been trying to get to eat all night.

"Oh fine. You guys have been giving each other lovey dovey eyes all night and kissed but you're not back together?" Stevie questioned as she turned her bathroom light off and joined me in her bedroom.

"I don't trust him Stevie he broke my heart before. He did it once I am sure he can do it again if I let him in. So, to keep from being broken by him it is best if we don't get back together. Plus, I am with Sebastian now and I adore him I never had to hide myself from him. Plus, those ice blue eyes and that blonde shaggy hair he pulls back is so fun to wrap my fingers in when we kiss."

She cuts me off, "okay but you two keep being on again and off again and I know how much that has hurt you."

"Yes, well… that is different he has a reason he has been trying to find Merlin plus sealing the evil things away and plus law school." I defended and really that was a big reason for it. "But yes, he is an amazing kisser." We sat laughing on the bed painting each other's nails like we were in high school again.

"But really who is better Sebastian or James?" She asked with a mischievous smile.

"Honestly Sebastian. James was amazing but I think it was more of a thrill of getting caught in the act and the wine talking but with Sebastian it is different... we have never had sex. He always wanted to wait until he is wed, he has always respected me and my body." I tell her thinking about Sebastian with a smile. "He excites me even without the sex."

"Oh, girl you're falling hard for him." She says with a big smile on her face as we blow on our nails to let them dry.

"I am but I still care about James, I loved him more than I should have let myself and honestly at the time I didn't even know what love was and I don't know if he truly ever loved me. I never told him or admitted it and maybe I should have but I didn't, and in some ways, I feel like he used me and took advantage of my feelings for him. I won't let him do that again." I let out a sigh and shook my head then looked at my nails. "I love the color black." Stevie puts a hand on my knee, and we make eye contact. I could tell she was worried about me so I gave her a confident smile, "don't worry I will be okay."

"Are you sure? Maybe you should tell James how you truly feel. Surely, he would listen, and you would find some closure." She replied and gave her nails a look over. "So do I." She giggled and blew a little more on them.

No, I wasn't sure about how things ended before, but I didn't tell her that I only gave her a soft smile and spoke. "Yes, I'm sure. I'm with Sebastian now we may not be Facebook official but we're together and that makes me happy. Plus, he doesn't have any type of social media anyways."

She smiles at me, but I could still see uncertainty in her eyes, but I didn't acknowledge it.

As Stevie and I continued to gossip we didn't know we was being listened to. A knock at the door broke us from our conversation.

"Come in." Stevie said from the bed and the door opens showing James on the other side of it. "Is everything okay?" Asked Stevie puzzled by his presence.

"Yes...I just...wondered if I could have a word with Stella?" He looks over at me kind of serious.

I get up off her bed and walk over to him looking back over my shoulder at her with a confused look.

"What do you want?" I questioned with a confused look still on my face.

"Can we talk in private?" He looks over my shoulder to Stevie sitting on the bed still listening to us as she acted like she was reading her Cosmo.

I sigh heavily and lead us out of her room into the hall. He pulls the door behind him and turns to me, "look we keep not getting to finish our conversation so can we go somewhere more private to talk?"

I think for a moment deciding against it, "no we can talk right here. What must be said won't take long.

We're never getting back together. Okay? That ship has sailed."

"Look I know I messed up but if you just give me a second…"

I cut him off in mid-sentence, "no James, no."

He scoffs. "What, does that uptight Sebastian guy have that I don't?"

"You listened in on our conversation!" I raised my voice furiously at him. I shove him. I shouldn't have but I shoved him, "what the hell is wrong with you?"

Stevie comes to the door and looks between us, "is everything okay?" About the moment Chester comes down the hall wondering the same thing.

"Yes, James was just going back to his room." I storm off back into the bedroom.

"I am going to go check on her. James it is best you just call it a night and leave her alone. You're not together anymore and you need to just accept that." She turns and closes the door and comes over and sits on the bed with me. "Want to talk about it?"

"No… no not really. I'm just pissed that he has the audacity to even think I would want to get back together with him. It isn't like things with Sebastian…. That is different… Sebastian never broke my heart. We have both always been so busy with school and other things that we knew we wouldn't have time for a relationship. That is why him and I stay on and off. Things with him are just different and just always feel right and I know, no matter what I will always go back to him…" I look down at my phone of pictures saved of us and smile.

Stevie looks at me and smiles nudging me, "you so love Sebastian, and I can tell for a fact he loves you.

Why don't you guys just admit it to each other and get married already?"

I looked at her shocked. "Stevie!"

"What? You know you have already planned your wedding I saw your board on Pinterest." She laughs at the expression on my face as I turn bright red.

"You're not funny." I tried to say without laughing but couldn't hold my amusement in. I knew she was right, and I couldn't deny it. Even if I tried, I would have been lying to myself. I knew the love I had for Sebastian was a love that ran deeper than anything I felt before. I felt connected to him on so

many levels both magically and romantically. For years even in high school we stayed drawn to each other, but I always thought we would be nothing more than star crossed lovers forever wondering this universe never finding the same passion that was felt when together.

Stevie snaps her fingers bringing me out of my daze. "Hey, hoe snap out of it."

I laugh, "you're such a bitch." I hit her with a pillow playfully.

"Are you ready for bed or are you going to stay awake daydreaming about lover boy?" She smiles and bats her eyes at me.

I roll my eyes at her and get under the covers, "oh shut up."

She turns off the light and comes to get in bed laughing at the fact I stuck my tongue out at her like a child would.

October 21, 2021

That morning you could feel the fall in the New England air as we got ourselves ready with her upstairs bedroom window open. The smell of the fresh fall leaves filled the bedroom, and the colors of the trees painted the forest around her house with burnt orange, golden yellows and bright reds. It was like looking outside at a painting. Her room always had the best view in the house to me. It was much like my room at my parent's home. They're never around much now because they've been enjoying traveling but when they're home, I visit as much as I can. I do miss them when they're away.

"Hey Stella, did you ever call Victoria?" I snap out of my daze and pull my sweater on.

"No, I sent her a text and she had said the fairies have been conversing with the trees and the trees are saying darkness is coming and it is coming fast."

"We need to start acting fast otherwise more humans and magick kind will die." Stevie's face falls as she closes her eyes trying to think. We hear a knock at her bedroom door and Chester comes in.

"Um did we say come in?" She teased him.

"Oh, please I've seen both of you naked more times than I can count." He said teasingly as he walked over to Stevie taking her in his arms kissing her playfully all over her face. He looks up at me, "by the way a ruggedly handsome blonde guy is here for you." He winked at me, and I felt my face light up and I take off running down the hall and down the stairs.

I see Sebastian standing at the door when he looks up to see me running and jumping into his arms wrapping my legs and arms around him. He laughs and catches himself before he falls over.

"Well, I missed you too." His kiss is warm and tender as one of his hands moves to my cheek and into my wavy red hair.

"Well, it looks like you found each other." Chester said jokingly.

We look up to see Stevie, Chester and James looking at us from the grand staircase. James's face was that of disgust whereas Chester and Stevie were amused at us.

"Don't we always?" Sebastian said sitting me down but still held me close. I look up at him lovingly happy that he was finally here.

"Now, I heard you needed an expert reader and enchanter on black magick and magical objects." Sebastian said picking back up his bags, "where should I set up?"

"Right this way." We, follow Stevie into the library to let Sebastian get sat up. He pulls out crystals, a small cauldron, opened a chest that had hundreds of bottles of potions. It was like he brought his whole house just about it.

"Sebastian I am pretty sure you brought everything but the kitchen sink." Chester said looked at his setup.

Sebastian laughed as he checked through to make sure he hadn't forgotten anything, "well we're dealing with evil, and we don't know what to expect. There is already a traitor among us all, so I am not going to go easy on them. Even if that means using black magick again. Hey don't touch that." He grabs a bottle out of James hand. "Who are you anyways?" Giving him a suspicious look of distrust.

"I am James, Stella's..." James went to reply.

I cut him off

"Remember the teacher I told you I dated?"

"Yeah?" Sebastian gave a side glance to James.

"That's him." I said with a hint of discomfort as I watched Sebastian's posture and expression.

"Why is he here?" Sebastian demanded coldly.

"Remember the student teaching program I am doing?" I questioned.

"Uh...yeah? That started already?" He ran his fingers through his head full of blonde curly wavy hair and looked back at me for more answers.

"Yes, anyways. Well long story short one of his students is a Calaway and his cult had us attacked at the end of the school day so now we're here." I still was not sure if that was the case or not or even if they were involved but it was the best beat that I had.

He looks at James his eyebrows raised and turns to look at me, "I'm gone

looking for Merlin and you get yourself into trouble. I can't leave you, alone, can I?"

I smile at him and bat my eyes, "whatever do you mean?"

He rolls his eyes and gets to work setting up a protection spell around the house and property.

"Well Sebastian! We didn't hear you come in dear, how was your trip?" Phoebe asked as her and Luke came into the library.

She walks over to him and gives him a hug and Luke shakes his hand.

"Welcome back son, how is your parents?"

"The trip was eventful and they're doing well. Alright that should keep out anyone that isn't welcomed and keep out anyone trying to listen in on what the plan will be to handle the Calaway's or whomever is involved." Sebastian flipped through one of the books that he had as he kept his mind focused.

"Good we need to act fast.... another witch was killed last night after the meeting... It was Sara."

Stevie and I gasp at Luke's words.

"No!" We both said at the same time.

"She would have never hurt anyone she was so free spirited." I said as I felt my eyes start to sting with wanting to cry.

"Who is Sara? Did I teach her?" James held shock and worry in his voice.

"No, James. Do you remember the women dancing last night?" I worked to calm down and felt Stevie rub my arms. We were both trying to not cry.

"Yes..." He replied remembering them.

"Sara was the beautiful girl with the pink hair and had a flower crown on." I explained. She had just dyed her hair the day before. She was so excited when she sent me a Snapchat of her hair and that silly pose she was doing.

We all fall silent. At loss for words because it is like we keep falling behind on protecting everyone we care about.

"What do we do now?" James asked.

"We call everyone that is on our side and let them know what is going on here and the progress we're making now that we have Sebastian home. With him here we won't be stopped. Not anymore. Our light magick is powerful but we need to catch them off guard. They will never know what hit them with us having the use of dark objects." Luke says seriously. "I never wanted it to come to this.... To have to use dark magick or dark objects to fight this war, but it seems that we're going to have to. At least long enough for them to think it is one of their own turning on them."

He walks off as he pulls out his phone to start making calls.

"Luke is just worried; he is our coven leader, and he feels responsible for everything that is happening." Phoebe said softly to us. "The royals may uphold the law, but our covens are our family."

"Dad is a good and fair leader mom, none of this is his fault. He tried to keep the peace and the other covens wouldn't comply. He must know that. Right?" Stevie said holding her mom's soft dainty hands.

"Yes dear, but that still doesn't stop him from feeling guilty. For all the wicked things that have been going on. Dark magick was always taught should only ever be used for evil or wicked ways and now this war has been brought to us all and we have only three choices…. Fight, join the darkness or die." She looks at us all her eyes going dark.

A cold chill runs down my spine thinking about everything that has happened in just a year. I look over at Sebastian who got back to work on making protection charms and whatever else was running through his mind to make to help us fight and keep us all safe. That worried me the most. I knew he would become their main target to kill because he is so powerful and because he is our only hope to stop this war now that Merlin is missing or gone. We can only hope the other immortals can find him. If who they say is back really or almost close, then surely Merlin is as well. Sebastian knows this and I can tell. I walk away holding back tears that I feel burning my eyes. Stevie walks up behind me and places a hand on my shoulder and leads us to the sunroom. There I let the tears run down my face. We both sit there in silent as I cry quietly till, I bring myself to stop.

"Now, I think I can guess what is troubling you. It's what Sebastian is doing isn't it? I remember earlier this year my dad and him was talking…. that him doing this would be the last resort because they knew how much danger it would put him in. You're scared for him, aren't you?" Her voice was soft and gentle as she spoke to me and took my hand holding it. Her eyes held a worried look that matched mine.

I look up at her wiping the tears from my eyes. "Yes, why does it have to be him? Why did he have to go and become this amazing witch? Why was it his family line that was led to do this for centuries? Why did Merlin have to have Sebastian be the one to do it? Why did Merlin leave us?"

She hands me a tissue and gives me a soft look, "it wouldn't be him if he didn't. You love him because he is this selfless amazing strong witch. As for his family… it seems like the Cameron bloodline has always been a long

line of knights and then lawyers that has only ever fought for what is right a just. Merlin… you know he had to do what he could, and thought would save us all. We can only hope he will come back. We need him."

I sigh and take the tissue to dry my eyes. "Yes, I know. Doesn't mean I have to like that he is risking his life over all of this."

"I don't like it either. That is why for all of use, all the good, that we must stop the evil before it spreads and kills anymore. I don't know how but we have to." Stevie looked out the window at the woods behind her home. "We have to… with or without Merlin."

I freshen myself up in the half bath downstairs checking to see if it looked to obvious that I didn't just have a meltdown. I felt my phone vibrate and it was a text from Victoria. I opened the message and read what it had said. Quickly coming out of the half bath and running into the library to everyone.

"Hey! Listen, Victoria just text and you guys are going to want to hear this." I pause to catch my breath because I am slightly out of shape but anyways, I opened the message again to read it to everyone, 'Stella we just got word from some animals and trees (yes I know it sounds crazy so hold that sarcastic attitude of yours for later) about something that happened last night with the demons. Two of them kidnapped some innocent college girls off campus. They used their compulsion on them. They took them back to their cult. Most of it you can figure out what exactly they did with the girls but what is even worse is it wasn't just the night walkers in the woods last night it was all the darkness we are up against. After they had their way with those girls, they used their human blood as a sacrifice in some dark spell. Sebastian might know what spell it is but whatever it was it wasn't good, and they told the demons, night walkers or whatever they are called but it was to bring them more to finish this spell so it can have its full power. Stella this is getting worse than we ever could imagine. They're already attacking the humans and using them.' This isn't good." I said after reading everything. I could tell the text was rushed. I couldn't even bring myself to laugh at the little joke she threw in to lighten the mood but even that did not help to lighten anything. "What now?"

I look up at everyone in the library and they all had pure shock on their faces. All but James. I didn't say anything about it. I am guessing at this

point he can't be shocked anymore by what is going on.

Overnight his world and everything he thought was real and pretend was flipped upside down. He just shook his head and rubbed his eyes. Everyone was silent. Stevie's mom was crying into Luke's arms and Stevie just stood there with shock. Chester left the room, but we heard something break out of anger in the next room and he said some choice words. I looked at Sebastian and he looked back at me. His eyes went dark, and I could tell he knew exactly what spell they were casting.

"Sebastian… What are they doing?" I asked him to break the deafening silence that was over the room.

Everyone turns to look at him. He stood with his hands on the table looking down at one of his books Argon had supplied him with his teeth gritted together.

"This spell was to never be used. Ever again. It was banned from even the darkest of warlocks back in the 12th century. It is called Nisi Tenebrae. Which translate to Only Darkness. A powerful immortal named Areses tried to cast this spell it took forces from light and dark magick to defeat him the last time this spell was in the works. It almost consumed everything in darkness when the spell was being cast. Not one mortal soul was safe, not even magick kind. He tried to rule over everyone. None of us are safe and all that is left is the sacrifice is more fertile human girls and the sacrifice of a powerful witch, warlock, fairy so fourth and so on. From each coven of magick to fuel the spell. Areses didn't complete it because each coven band together to save one another. Some might have been for selfish reasons, but it saved us all from being wiped away from existence or being born into slavery centuries later, but it was Argon, Citrine, Agate and Carnelian with the guidance of Merlin that ultimately sealed him away."

Luke came up behind him and placed a hand on his shoulder, "I remember studying this when I was younger, but I never thought someone would do this type of dark spell ever again it was always rumored it was a myth, a folklore that surrounded Merlin…. Is he really gone? There is still no sign of him? Stella, did Victoria say who is the actual leader of this darkness?"

"There is nothing…. So far. The other immortals are still looking for him… sadly there is no clues to go from and Clara is still… let's just say she isn't like the Clara we all know. This event… all of this. It has changed her. She is quiet, depressed… it is hard to see her in such a state and too had to of watch her marry Prince Wesley." Sebastian replied sadly and let out a

heavy sigh as he reached into his suit pocket and pulled out his flask to take a swig of it. "Wesley is good to her though and patient, but he knows she does not love him… at least not the way she loves Daniel… Merlin, hell I do not know what to call him. Growing up we always called him Daniel and now suddenly we find out he is Merlin." He shakes his head and lets out a shaky breath.

"Yes, and it is someone I never thought would turn on everyone. The Calaway's aren't even involved with them. Yes, they're not the nicest but they're not the ones killing everyone." I chime in to try and change the sad subject with answering the question. "I had it all wrong."

"Well get to it who is behind this?" Chester cuts in as he walks back into the room.

"Rosalleta." I whispered sadly.

A few of them gasped as they heard her name. A girl who everyone thought was beautiful and kind. A girl who just last night was dancing with Sara who turned up dead this morning. Someone we never thought would ever harm anyone in her life. Someone on many occasions I would dance and kiss by the river all day and night and some nights would go too far with. My heart broke reading her name on my screen.

"We don't know for sure if it is her or if someone is using her as a vessel. Right? She could just be under a spell." Stevie said quickly not wanting to believe that our friend would ever do something like this.

Sebastian rubbed his temple, "that is true, she could just be a vessel for someone. An innocent face for others to fall for and join. Her magick isn't strong. This spell needs someone very powerful and Rosalleta is not a powerful enough witch to handle such a spell."

I sigh with relief hearing that but worried about who has her and what will happen to her after all of this.

"Whoever has her is using her as a shield so we can't spy on them or see them coming. It is a very clever trick. I don't know how long whoever it is will use her before they get tired of her." Sebastian walked over to one of the big windows in the library and looked out thinking when something flies towards him aiming to kill. The protection spell defended him, but it got all our attention.

I ran over to him wrapping my arms around him with my head on his chest I could feel his heartbeat pounding on the inside but on the outside, he showed no fear. "Are you okay?" I took his face in my hands feeling a tear run down my cheek. He smiled at me and wiped the tear from my face.

"Yes, I planned for something like this to happen that is why I put up a protection spell. Don't cry, I'm okay." He pulls me into him and kisses the top of my head. I hold on to him tightly never wanting to let go afraid if I do, I will lose him. "You need to text Victoria and tell her everything you have learned, and we need to warn the others and to be prepared for what is coming."

I nod and pull reluctantly away from him as I text Victoria of the newfound information for her to get out to her people. "Okay, she is spreading the word. What do we do next?"

"Dad is calling the Calaway's... He is going to try and make peace with them so they can help fight this Darkness. He is telling them everything we have learned." Stevie said coming back into the room that I didn't even know she had left from.

"Can we trust them?" Chester asked from his place on the red velvet couch by the grand fireplace.

"I don't think we have much of a choice given the circumstances. Any other day I would say no, but I would rather face what wicked they have planned for later than what we are facing right now." Stevie said as she took her spot next to Chester curled up on the couch by the fire.

"Well, I am tired of just sitting here. Why aren't we out there right now fighting whatever it is that needs to be fought? It's like we're part of some lame ass book that is taking forever to get to the fighting and problem solving." Chester stated in aggravation.

"Chester. We can't just run out there blindly in a fit of rage to fight this thing. That is how we will get killed. Plus, they're waiting for us. They already attacked the house knowing we have a protection spells up but did it to let us know they're here and they're watching us. If we run out there now without a game plan and without backup, then we're all dead. So yes, we are the boring part of some book waiting for the fighting because we're trying to not get killed in the process of coming up with the best defense for the all-out war that is coming." Stevie scolded him from her spot next to him on the couch, her arms crossed over her chest giving him a stern look like she was addressing a small child who was having a tantrum.

I let out a laugh looking at the two of them because he went from looking pissed off to ashamed of himself in five seconds' flat. They turn and look at me and we all laugh together.

"Don't worry Chester you will get to fight. It might be sooner rather than

later." Sebastian said from his spot back in front of the table looking into his cauldron.

"What do you mean?" We all quickly moved over to where he was.

"Momma, Dad! Come in here." Stevie yelled. They came rushing over to where we all stood.

"What I mean is… they're bringing the war to us… If not tonight, then soon. Look." He said nodding to his cauldron.

We all look inside and see flashes of what's to come. My heart sinks in my chest as I see flashes of all of us in battle and some of us hurt and friends and others we know falling at the hands of pure evil. Sebastian had picked up that little trick from Argon and it never failed or showed anything false. Luke broke the silence and our thoughts, "That settles it, I'm calling a meeting tonight. Sebastian, I need you to extend the protection spell on the property so we can get everyone in here. The Calaway's are on board with helping fight this thing and said their cult will side with us. Just this once." He leaves the room and pulls out his phone and starts making phone calls and I text Victoria to spread the word about tonight to the rest of the fairies and others.

Sebastian sets to work on expanding the protection spell holding Stevie and I's hand to pull more power from to strengthen the wards and to only allow in those we let in.

"So, James, you've been awfully quiet about all of this. I would think a mere human would be going crazy right now." Chester said poking for questions.

"Chester lay off I know you're bored but don't go picking fights." I scold Chester. "Go eat you get cranky when you haven't eaten."

"It's quite aright Stella I am more than capable of defending myself. Chester quite frankly at this point there is nothing I can say or do here. I have no magick or powers to defend myself so there is no pointing and running because they know I am associated with all of you, so I am as good as dead. Now there is other humans being used in this horrible thing and I can't even help with that so what good am I other than sitting here and staying out of the way so things can get done." James sighs and ran his fingers through his hair dark hair.

"At least you know you're defenseless in case you try anything." Chester teased.

"Chester, layoff. This is a lot to take in for a person." Stevie said scolding

him.

"Alright, I know. I'm just bored." Chester said tossing up a small fireball and catching it as he laid down on the couch with a sigh. "I am hungry."

I giggle and spell up a water ball and drop it on Chester's head causing him to jump up shaking the water off.

"Stella!" Chester yelled and looked at me with an angry look.

Stevie and I hold each other laughing uncontrollably. He repays the favor to us as water dumps on our heads soaking us. The three of us look at each other and how ridiculous we looked and started back to laugh when we spelled up a drying spell to help each other dry off and back to normal.

"So, are you guys done playing so we can set up for the meeting tonight?" Sebastian asked leaning on the table that he had all his things on. I couldn't help but smile at him. His sleeves rolled up and him pushing his glasses back in place as his shaggy blonde hair feel in front of his blue eyes. Biting my lower lip, I went over and wrapped my arms around his neck and pulled him in for a kiss.

"Now I'm ready." I smiled pulling away looking up at him smiling back at me. "I love your eyes and smile. You know that?"

He pulls my hands up to his lips and kisses them and smiles at me. "And you're beautiful."

"Okay, are you guys done being all lovey dovey and shit?" Chester teased acting like he was about to throw up.

"Chester stop being a dick," Stevie laughed, "they haven't seen each other in months because of his trip so I think they're definitely due for some way overdue bedroom time."

"Stevie!" My face and Sebastian's turn fifty shades of red as she held her side from laughing at our red-faced expressions.

"Well, I am glad to see everyone is in a good mood, but the others are showing up. We need to gather and start the meeting." Phoebe said standing in the doorway smiling at us.

Still holding my hand in his he pulls me into the large den with him and the others where Stevie's dad stood in the middle with the other leaders of each clan. I spot Victoria coming over to us her cute curvy figure filling out her flowy purple dress and her long brown hair with flowers all in it to match.

"Stella! Stevie!" Victoria rushed to us excitedly.

"Victoria!" We both said at the same time.

We embrace each other, glad to see that we were all safe.

"Did you all make it in safely? No trouble?" Stevie questions.

"Yes, Sebastian's spell is really powerful. You feel it from miles. I don't

think any of the dark magick can get in." She looks at Sebastian, "it is so good to have you back, we need you."

Sebastian nods his head at her, "I will do everything I can to stop this."

I look at the ground suddenly feeling sick to my stomach from the thought of something horrible happening to him. Not knowing if I could live though it if something did. The meeting goes on and I am zoned out, not hearing a word that is said because I am lost in my own thoughts knowing that is just selfish of me when there is so much more on the line. I can only think of one thing is that I can't stand by and let Sebastian risk his life. The only way I can help anyone and be at my best would be if we broke up again otherwise, I would spend more time thinking and worrying about him being away fighting and wondering if he was coming home.

Sebastian looks down at me seemingly knowing what I was thinking with a sad but knowing expression on his face that it probably is for the best right now even if it isn't. He kisses my hand one last time and looks into my eyes as if telling me it will be okay, and he will come back. He walks to the middle of the room with the other Elders to address every one of the evils we are facing and the vision he saw, as he replayed the vision above us all from of his crystal ball. Gasp of horror come from everywhere around me and children start to cry.

"Stella?" Victoria spoke softly to me, "are you and Sebastian, okay?"

I look at her as a silent tear runs down my face, "we just broke up again."

"Oh honey." She pulls me in for a hug and strokes the back of my hair. "It will be okay. You two always find your way back to each other. You have since you found each other when you were in high school. You both are forces to always be drawn together. You are each other's twin flame." Her country accent sounding just a bit more southern than it normally did.

Unfortunately, it always feels like things pull us apart. I pull away from Victoria and all I can see is my beautiful blonde-haired blue-eyed love of my life. Although we have never said the words "I love you" to each other I could always feel how much love he has always felt for me and I him. He looks back at me as the images play above us all and slowly turn to darkness. I see how much he is hurting on the inside from just looking into his eyes and it makes me feel even more sick to my stomach and my heart feel like it's being ripped from my chest. It has never hurt this bad before when we had split up in the past. Tonight, it is different. Tonight, it is like we're saying goodbye forever. It is like he is holding back something and knowing how the ending will be and isn't telling anyone but from reading

his eyes I know how it will end and it ends with him dying to save us all. My heart can't handle it and I quietly leave the room finding my way back to the sunroom to let out a loud sob I have been holding in. Holding my sides and crying to the point of making myself sick.

Stevie and Victoria find me curled up on the couch in the sunroom looking like a hot mess.

"Stella, sweetie. What happed?" Stevie asked as she sat down next to me and Victoria on the other said.

I choke on a sob, "Sebastian and I broke up… again because of everything going on and because he knows he will end up dying."

"We don't know that for sure. Things could change and all this crying will be over nothing. Don't jump to the worst possible conclusion. Even if he is doing it thinking it will protect you." Victoria spoke to me softly playing with my hair.

40

I calm myself down after talking to them and get back to feeling somewhat better but still heartbroken.

"Hey! Why don't we have an actual sleepover like we did last year? We haven't had one since then because of all this going on! We're locked in my parent's house together anyways so why not take up the opportunity and play some old school music from when we were teenagers and some of our favorite songs now and eats junk food and pizza and..." Stevie was so excited that Victoria and I started laughing.

"Calm down. You're talking so fast." Victoria teased her.

"It all sounds like fun, let's go to the kitchen and get everything we need for a night of fun and plus we cannot forget the wine!" I said jumping up starting to get back to my old self after my moment of being my overly dramatic self.

We head off into the kitchen just off the sunroom and start getting everything we wanted to eat. We popped two pizzas in the big oven and gathered the rest of what we wanted.

"Um... so how are we going to get all of this up to your bedroom?" We noticed we had way more to take up than we had arms to hold it all.

"Hold on! I got an idea." Stevie runs off and comes back with her laundry basket and starts putting all the chips, salsa, guacamole, a big bowl of popcorn, two bottles of red wine and two bottles of white, cookies, and strawberries with chocolate dip and the glasses for the wine. The pizzas finished and we put them on trays to take up to Stevie's bedroom.

We get up to her room ready for our night to enjoy ourselves. Stevie turned on her Bluetooth and grabbed my phone. "Let's see what is on this playlist of yours now." I rolled my eyes and took a bite of pizza, "ah! You have the

song Year 3000 by the Jonas Brothers!" She got excited and started to play it putting my phone on random so they would get a kick out of my playlist that really was random as hell. Thank you, Spotify.

We sang along to the song as we ate and drank our wine. "Okay, so let's make a game out of the songs. Next song that comes up we say who the song reminds us of from past and now boyfriends." Victoria said as the song started to finish up. I could tell she was already getting a slight little buzz, but we all were.

The song Crazy in Love by Nicole Andersson that was in Fifty Shades of Grey starts to play and Victoria gets excited and starts the game she made up. "Oh, oh, oh yes I go first! For me the song would have to remind me of David. Stevie you're next."

"Obviously Chester. You Stella?" Stevie replied and took a bite of pizza. They look at me and I rolled my eyes, "it should be obvious, Sebastian. Duh." We start to laugh enjoying ourselves as the game went on. Completely forgetting our problems and the war going on. Not knowing at that time there was someone working against us, someone we were supposed to be able to trust.

"Next song! Perfect by One Direction. Girl I forgot how much of a groupie you had been in school when it came to boy bands" Stevie teased and popped a strawberry in her mouth and giggled at my face.

I threw popcorn at Stevie, "shut up." I laughed, "that song would have to be dedicated to James. One of you guys is up."

"Ooooo, Mr. Kirkwood." Victoria said teasing me dancing with her shoulders and batted her lashes. "You both would flirt in class. I knew you would date him."

"Oh, hush and answer the question." I said shaking my head and laughing.

"Fine, I would have to say Robby if you guys remember him from high school." She lets out a sad sigh. I had almost forgot about him. I don't know how but she was crazy over him.

"Oh yeah, I forgot about him! Your parents really did not approve of him." I said as I watched her shrug.

"Lord, I remember that time you snuck out of my house to go out and meet him in our woods just to see him." Stevie teased her.

"Okay, okay, Stevie it is your turn." Getting off the subject of herself.

"Humm, if you guys remember Liam from high school, this song would fit him I would say." Stevie took a sip of her wine to wash down the strawberry and chocolate.

That song ends and another starts, "Back to You by Selena Gomez, Victoria

you first."

She thinks for a moment. "Honestly there isn't anyone I would go back to." Stating in a matter-of-fact voice.

"Same for me," Stevie says, "you Stella?"

"Sebastian. I'll always go back to him. No matter what." I down my wine and look at the girls who have smiles on their faces. "What?"

"You guys are so going to get married." Stevie says and Victoria nodding in agreement.

We hear a thud outside the door and turn to look at it. With a flick of Stevie's wrist, she opens the door to see all three of the guys at the door and Chester on the ground from obviously falling over and James scolding him for being too loud. They realize we caught them and are looking at them as we sit on the bed drinking our wine. They slowly turn to look at us, all three pales as ghost.

"So, care to explain why you guys were ease dropping in on us?" Stevie said playing with fire that she spelled up in her hand as she kept looking at the boys.

"Uh, well, um… you see. We… James?" Chester looks to James for some back up.

"Don't look at me this was your idea." He puts his hands up in defense.

"Sebastian, can I get some back up?" Chester turns to him, and Sebastian's face turns red.

"Well," he closes his eyes and scratches the back of his head and gives and embarrassed laugh, "please don't kill us."

The girls and I smile at how embarrassed the guys are for getting caught.

"So…. Can I have some pizza?" Chester looked over and the pizza on the bed and licked his lips then back down at his lover who looked at him in amusement.

"In your little failed detective work did you learn anything?" Stevie asked them still wilding the fireball she kept tossing up and catching like a baseball.

Chester and the boys kept eyeing the fireball anticipating when she would throw it at them. The fun was short lived as an explosion from outside shook the manner and screams came from the north wing of the house. We jump up off the bed in shock frozen looking at one another.

"You boys go check on everyone. We need to quickly change clothes." Victoria ordered them. They nodded and run off without another word.

We all quickly change. I pulled on my black sports bra and black tank-top pulling on a camo dry fit jacket, and I pulled out my matching camo running pants. I put my rucksack on that had everything in it that I took with me for emergencies and the girls did the same with suiting up for battle. We looked at each other and held hands silently praying that this wouldn't be the last time we saw each other and that our time together wasn't coming to an end. "I love you guys, this is it, are you both ready?" I spoke and took in a deep breath.

"I love you guys too." Victoria said with a small smile on her lips, "let's go kick some bad guy ass."

"I'll love you both forever, let's go show them what these three girls are made of." Stevie said with confidence.

We all smiled and left Stevie's room with confidence and ran to where all the screaming was going on. We see the Calaway's in battle with other witches from another coven. Their son is quite impressive moving with grace and speed taking out his opponents without breaking a sweat. Stevie's parents aren't far from them holding their own back-to-back working together feeding off each other's magick to bring those down that broke through. I break out of my daze and a fireball narrowly misses me. I turn my attention to a wild haired witch with a thirsty look on her face.

"Well, well, well little witch does she think she can play with the big boys?" She smiled showing her rotten teeth at me, "where is that boyfriend of yours. The boss needs him. Dead or alive but they'd rather have him alive."

"What do you want with Sebastian?" I send back a spell. This time I am pissed, and I can feel my anger bubbling up in me and reaching my fingertips as I send off another spell that sends her flying into a pile of rubble from the destroyed northern wing of the house. She struggles to get up, pissed off but I don't give her a moment to think as I hold out my hand chanting a spell that causes her to not be able to breathe. *"Nec de Resp."* My magick raises her up above me and I feel the darkness of my magick starting to consume me from all my anger. I drop her and stand over her giving her a moment to answer my question. "I will ask again what do they want with Sebastian?"

She looks up at me catching her breath, "to sacrifice him to complete the spell. Sebastian is a Cameron and the Cameron's spent centuries sealing away demons and other forms of what they call night walkers. If he is killed and his blood is spilled ending the Cameron bloodline then everyone him and his ancestors have sealed away will be set free."

"Who are you working for?" I asked heatedly.

She smiles up at me wickedly, "you haven't figured it out, yet have you?"

"What are you talking about?" I look at her confused as the battle rages on and enemy and allies alike falling. "Who are you working for?"

Stevie and Victoria run up to me while I am questioning this witch, "Stella let's go we need to keep moving." They both say.

"Hold on. Who is it? Tell me!" I shouted.

She smiles at me, "you went from being his student to be his lover. Your love for him you still have over him clouded your thoughts. You didn't even notice that he is your enemy." She starts to laugh the most horrible, wicked laugh I had ever heard.

Stevie quickly killed her as I stood there in shock.

"No, she has to be lying. James... he can't be. We would have known... I would have known. It has to be a mistake." I look at both Victoria and Stevie as rubble falls around us and the cries of people dying in battle. "Then Merlin... what of Merlin? Oh God Clara...."

"Stella, we need to keep moving we're an open target standing here. We will find out what is going on and what is the truth and a lie in plenty of time." Victoria said pulling me to move as Stevie throws up a shield around us as more rubble falls.

I shake my head finding my thoughts knowing that they're right. If I keep letting my feelings get in the way I will end up dead. I nod at them, and we take off running and come across Gabriel holding his own. Another warlock comes up behind him and tries to attack him while he is warding off two other warlocks. I send off a spell breaking the neck of the guy behind him. Gabriel kills the other two and looks at us.

"Thank you for that," he straightens out his sports jacket and tie that he still had on from the meeting earlier that he had yet to get to change out of. He looked hot, and I could tell Victoria was undressing this guy with her bedroom eyes.

"Pretty impressive, I'm Victoria," she held out her hand, "I don't think we have met."

He took her hand and brought it to his lips and kissed her knuckles, "Gabriel, Gabriel Calaway. The pleasure is all mine."

Victoria blushed and I rolled my eyes at them. "Okay kids we have got to keep going or we will end up dead and I need to find Sebastian before he ends up a blood sacrifice by Mr. Kirkwood."

We all take off together, "wait there is something you need to know about Kirkwood," Gabriel said, "that is not the real James."

"Wait, what?" All three of us said as we kept moving and kept fighting alongside each other.

"My parents knew something was wrong with him. I got placed in his class for a reason and it was to keep an eye on him. They knew that the darkness that was coming was going to target everyone we cared about. The James you saw in class Stella was the real James. The one with you now is not him. A changeling took his place when he came to your door the other night. James is still safe my parents put an enchantment on him and put him in a coma like state to have him admitted to the hospital for his own safety. The one posing as him is another minion of Areses. We need to keep playing off like we think that is James. If not, he will turn into someone else, and we will be out of luck and not know who to trust." Gabriel said to us very seriously.

"Why were none of us told about this?" I asked in pure shock.

"We didn't want the word to get out and our cover get busted. My family really isn't that bad." He says shrugging his shoulders and taking out a guy behind me.

"Thanks." I say repaying the favor.

The fighting goes on like this for hours till the wards are put backup. We were able to find Sebastian and Chester again and we can tell they had also been through hell.

"Who restored the ward and how did they break it?" I ask.

"I put it back up. It wasn't easy while being attacked but Chester had my back. We lost James though. I don't know where he is, and we have a lot of bodies to go through." Sebastian said looking around at all the death and destruction that had happened that night. "I hope he isn't among the dead."

"How did the ward get broken Sebastian?" Victoria asked.

"I don't know. I thought… I thought I made sure there was no way it could be broke…" He looks down in disappointment at himself. I could tell he blamed himself for this even though it wasn't his fault.

"Sebastian… none of this is your fault. Whatever we are facing is stronger than any of us could have ever imagine." I walk over to him and take his hands in mine, and he meets my eyes. I move my hands from his and take

his face between them and lean in slowly to kiss him. I feel him wrap his arm around me pulling me close to him. I hear our friends whistle and carry on like children aggravating us, but we kept kissing until we had to pulled away to catch our breath.

"Okay, now that we have that done let's find the survivors and the injured." Chester said leading the way.

We walk around checking and helping those that were injured and making a hospital unit in the ballroom area of the manner. Stevie's parents had already been setting up for it along with Gabriel's. Lucky for us all Mrs. Calaway and Luke happened to be surgeons and Phoebe was a nurse at the same hospital they worked at. They all three got down to business treating everyone we brought in and those that wasn't hurt helped them by doing as they said and bringing what they needed or helped bring in the wounded.

"This was just the first attack. We lost a lot of lives today. Classmates we went to school with, and Gabriel lost kids he was in school with. What are we going to do?" Stevie whispered to me as we lay out the dead bodies and wrote down the names of those we had lost.

"Stella! Stevie! Over here!" We stopped what we were doing and ran over to Chester.

"What is it...?" Stevie asked and her voice trailed off and we looked down to see the body of James or who was meant to be James.

"Stella. I am so sorry." Chester said with remorse in his eyes. Stevie and I looked at each other wondering if we should let him in on what we had learned or not.

"Chester, there is something we have to tell you." I said as we sat him down on a nearby bench. We both spoke in very hushed tones so no one could hear us. After we finished his expression was hard. "So, what are you thinking?" I asked looking at him waiting for an answer.

He contemplates for a moment. "I think we need to tell the others."

"I agree with Chester. We could have others that are posing as trusted people." Stevie nodding in agreement with Chester. She crossed her arms over her chest and her brow furrowed together as she was thinking. "Why did Gabriel not say anything till now or better yet why did his parents keep this information from everyone?"

"I think it was to keep everyone safe." I stated. "The less people that knew the safer they probably thought they was keeping all of us."

"I guess I can see that." Still sounding unsure about all of it Chester rubs his chin as he sat thinking. "Okay, enough standing around here let's get back to

the others." Chester got up and started heading to the ballroom where most everyone else was gathered. "I am starvin'." He grumbled.

We walk quietly back to the ballroom all lost in thought about what all happened and what is yet to come. Once we get back to everyone there is people grouped off and you can feel the sadness sinking in and the silent sobs of our fellow comrades. Agonizing screams of those finding our friends and loved ones who have died and will never get to see again. My chest tightened from feeling the pain of those around me. The pain was almost unbearable for me to take but I pulled myself together because I knew that I had to keep staying strong. This was only a preview of the death and destruction that was to come. Chester and Stevie walked off to her parents and I stood alone in the middle of the room surrounded by the injured, I feel Victoria walk up beside me. She has this positive energy that radiates off her, but she is so strong and skilled as a fighter. Most people think fairies are these small little magical things with wings that fly around like the ones in cartoons, but fairies are so much more than what is shown in the movies and TV shows. They're strong and skilled worriers like the elves. Both magical and both should never be underestimated, and it is so good that we have both on our side. And no not the little things running around at Santa's workshop either, if you have ever played Dungeons and Dragons then they have the closest recorded description of the true elves. Argon's children come from a long line of powerful elves that he created himself centuries ago, people of power envy the elves.
I look around and I spot Raven the girl from James class sitting with some other girl I recognized from that class. I grab Victoria's arm and lead her over there with me.
"Hey, Raven, right?" I called out to her.
She looked up when she heard my voice, "oh! Stella, hey I didn't know you were magical. Are you both witches too?"
Victoria and I look at each other and smile.
"No, I am a fairy." Victoria smiled at her and with a wave of her hand her beautiful angelic wings appear.
The three teenagers looked at her wings in awe and wonder.
"Your wings are so pretty!" They all said at different times.
Victoria smiled and blushed slightly. "Thank you, have you never seen fairy wings before?"
"No! We haven't even met a fairy that we know of." Raven said.
"Really? I thought some went to your school?" I questioned with a confused

look on my face.

"They may but we just don't know it. None of us talk about what we are or where we came from because it's too dangerous." Raven stated.

"What do you mean dangerous?" I asked.

"We just started going to public school this year and our parents told us to be careful and lay low, that it's dangerous for humans and magick kind now. Which they were right." She said and nodded her head towards the destruction.

We all went silent for a moment. Taking in everything that has happened within these short few days.

"It will get better. We will beat this and come back from it." Victoria said with confidence to us. "We just have to work together and believe in each other."

Sebastian walks over to us after talking with all the elders. He takes me in his arms and just holds me like that for what felt like forever.

"What is it?" I asked assuming something must be wrong.

"Nothing, I just needed to hold you again." He mummers into my hair to me still holding me and running his fingers through my fallen hair.

"But we broke up? Again." I responded.

"I know." He slowly pulled away from me and our eyes locked on each other. We were both dirty from the battle, but his blue eyes still shined brightly. He kissed my cheek and walked away to go talk to Chester.

"Who was that?" Raven asked eyes wide.

"That is Sebastian. The person who will save us all." I looked back over my shoulder, and he looked back at me.

"Why don't you guys just get back together? The whole on again off again and just randomly talking to each other or seeing each other is getting old. If you're not going to get back together then stay broke up and move on! Stop doing this to yourself. There are more guys than just him." Victoria blurted out. She covered her mouth, "oh, I'm sorry I shouldn't have gone off like that." I smiled back at her a sad smile.

"It's okay. You're right." I look back at him one last time before excusing myself back to Stevie's room.

Chapter 6

      I find myself back in Stevie's room getting my things together for a shower when Stevie and Victoria come in.

"Oh Stella, I am so sorry. I didn't mean to upset you. The whole situation just makes me so mad." Victoria said as she came over and sat on the end of the bed.

"No, it's okay, really. I'm fine." I said trying to sound confident with a small smile, "I'm going to go take a quick shower."

I went into the bathroom and closed the door. I felt a tear role down my cheek as I leaned up against the door. I close my eyes but images of his face and blue eyes seem to flood my mind. Parts of me wished I had never met him so I would never have to feel like this. I love him so much it hurts. It doesn't matter how bad I want to move on and how much I try I find myself longing for him every single time and thinking about him. No matter what I continue to want him. I pull myself away from the door to go over and start the shower. As the water warms up, I get undressed and grab a washcloth before stepping in the shower. I hear someone knock on Stevie's bedroom door and she answers it. I go to the door and press my ear to the door to listen.

"Hey, is Stella in here with you?" I recognize that voice anywhere and the sound of it pulls at my chest.

"Yes, but Sebastian…. You can't keep doing her like this. If you want to be with her then just be with her. The way you string her along and doing this on again off again bullshit is just that it is bullshit." I hear Stevie lay into him and it makes me smile a bit.

"I know. I do care about her I am just scared of the whole relationship and…" She cuts him off.

"Oh, drop the bullshit and grow the fuck up Sebastian. You're not in high

school. If you want her then prove it but if you're just going to pull another Houdini act and disappear on her after this war is over then you can go on ahead and remove yourself from her life. You're good at that. You know she would have never started dating James if it wasn't for you pulling another one of your stunts. She waited on you and that is all she has ever done. It doesn't matter how hard she tries to move on she always messes up her relationships because none of them can compare to you. Although James messed up theirs but that is beside the point. Look I will tell her you stopped by, but you need to go before I hex you because you piss me the fuck off." Before he can say anything else, she closes the door in his face.

I come away from the door and get in the shower and feel a small smile come across my face and a giggle because she really went off on him. She has always had my back even when she really didn't have to. I finish up my shower and get out drying myself off when Stevie knocks at the bathroom door.

"Sweetie how are you doing?" She calls from the other side.

"I'm fine. Just drying off and getting my pj's on." I get dressed and open the door to find her and Victoria on the other side waiting for me. The mess downstair still fresh in my mind. I knew we could not linger on it. We had to keep going. Keep pushing forward. I was tired and ready to give up on the whole day. It went from being a nice day to being what it was now.

"What is it?" I looked between them waiting for an answer.

"Sebastian came by and wants you to call or text him." Victoria blurted out.

"I know I heard everything from the bathroom. I'll give him a call I guess." I grab my phone from off the bed and press the call button next to his name. I feel my heart racing as the phone rings.

"Stella, hey…" I hear him answer and I feel like my heart is in my throat ready to jump out.

"Hey… you wanted me to call?" I respond quietly.

"Umm, well, yes, look I didn't mean to upset you, but I think for now it is best if we stay broken up until I figure out what I want. It isn't right for me to keep stringing you along. I care about you but so much is going on right now… I'm sorry Stella…" He got quiet and waited for me to respond.

I was silent and couldn't make words form on how I felt at that moment all I could manage to get out was, "Goodbye Sebastian…"

"Wait! Stella…" I hung up the phone before he could say anymore. My chest felt tight, and I thought I was going to die from a broken heart. I felt Victoria and Stevie come up behind me and gave me a group hug as I broke

down and cried.

I let my phone fall on the bed as I held my head in my hands and cried. We stayed quiet for what felt like an eternity.

"You know what we need to do?" Victoria said.

"What?" Asked Stevie and me.

"We need to actually go out and have some fun instead of being stuck in here. Why don't we get cleaned up and go to a club, have a few drinks and dance?" She said with a big smile on her face.

"I don't know Victoria. We just had a raging war go on. Do you really think we should get all sexy and go out?" Stevie had a hint of concern in her voice when she asked.

"Why not? We should go out before it is too late because we may never get this chance again to all be together. The war just proved that. The night is still young it's only 8 o'clock. Today just feels like a long day with everything that has happened." She responded very enthusiastically. "Plus, we can do some detective work."

"Well, I don't know… What do you think Stella?" Stevie looked at me unsure still if this was a good idea or not.

I thought about it and only could think about how I just need to get out and have a few drinks, "let's do it." I got up and start to get ready.

They looked at each other and started to get ready as well.

I went through all of Stevie's clothes and found a tight black dress that had a deep v-cut and showed cleavage, and my sky-high black leather boots I had left in her closet to match. I dried my hair then curled it. I applied my makeup making sure I didn't leave out the dark blood red lipstick. Stevie found her black ripped skinny jeans and her silky red tank top and her red high heels. She dolled herself up and I knew for a fact she would be turning some heads tonight. Victoria wasted no time in knowing what she was going to wear. I think she already had it in mind when she planned this outing. She had on her tight high waisted black leather skirt that showed off her curves and her purple lace bralette that showed off her bust area. Her hair and makeup were fixed to perfection like always. We looked hella hot. We hear a knock at the door and Stevie went and answered it. Raven and her two friends were on the other side.

"Raven, hey. What's up?" Stevie said.

"You guys are going out? Can we go to? We're so bored being locked up in

here." Raven asked, "I mean… aside from everything that happened… honestly we just want to not be around all the sadness and death." She frowns and looks down at the shoes.

"Sure but…" About that time Stevie's parents came walking up.

"Stevie where do you all think you're going? The only way you all can go is if Chester and Sebastian go with you for protection." Great that is just my luck. "Chester, Sebastian." Her dad knocks on their door.

Chester opens their door. "Hey what's going on?"

"You and Sebastian go with the girls tonight to protect them please. They thought they could sneak out and go without any of us knowing and they don't need to go without you boys." Her dad says. "Now I need to get to bed. Be safe and have fun." He walks away down the hall.

"Well fuck." I said as Stevie closes the door after Raven and her friends came in. "I wanted to get out and get my mind off things about Sebastian and now he is coming."

"We can still have fun! We don't have to stay around them and plus when he sees how drop dead gorgeous you look; he will totally regret ever breaking up with you." Victoria said as she grabbed her small purse. "Alright girls let's hit the dance floor and checkout hot boys!" She headed for the door, and we all followed. Her energy was magnetic, you couldn't help but get drawn to it. Where it came from, I did not know but it made us all feel better.

We met the boy's downstairs. Chester nudged Sebastian and nodded my way. Sebastian turns around and his eyes go wide, and his mouth drops as he watches me walk down the stairs. I keep myself together the best I can. I was drawn to him and how amazing he looked but I tried to not seem like I was checking him out. He had on a white V-neck T-shirt and a black leather jacket, and his dark denim ripped jeans with his black Converse. He looked amazing. It was different from the suits he always wore. I felt my cheeks start to blush lightly as his eyes stayed on me devouring me in his gaze. I could feel him mentally undressing me with his eyes. I bit my bottom lip and looked back into his fierce blue eyes and saw him lick his lips hungerly. He brushed his hand through his hair and forced himself to stop looking at me. I pull my eyes away from him also and walked out the door to Stevie's SUV.

"Okay, we are not all going to fit so we will have to take two different cars. Raven, you and your friends are with the girls and I. Boys you're going in

another car, oh and I had dad to tell Gabriel to go along with you guys. He will be along shortly. Here he is now." She looks behind them to see Gabriel coming down the steps to the outside.

"Well, let's get this party started, shall we?" He said walking up and checking me out in the process, "by the way ladies you all look ravishing." He took my hand and kissed it then opened my car door for me offering to help me in.
"Oh, thank you." I blushed and got in the front seat.
"Of course." He bows his head to me, "now, we do have a stop to make. Mother dear has awakened James and request that we fetch him from the hospital. She has explained everything to him and is sending him with us to keep us out of trouble." You have got to be fucking kidding me I thought to myself as he closed my car door. "Mother had the liberty of taking all those hurt and killed taken to the hospital with the help of a bit of hocus pocus. She is there treating everyone." He explained.

We all load up and head out to the hospital to pick up James and I was already regretting agreeing to going out. I mean yeah, I need the time out and plus we can investigate the night life and see just what has been going on with the night walkers but having both my exes tagging along isn't exactly my ideal idea of a night out.

We pull into the hospital, and I see James standing by the hospital entrance waiting for us. He walked over to Chester's window and said something to him, but I obviously couldn't hear them. After a few moments he gets in the back seat and we're on the road again to Sivas Night Club. Stevie hooks her phone up to her Bluetooth in her car and plays her playlist on random to get us in the mood to party. After a moment I lighten up and let the fact go that I'm stuck with two of my exes on this night out. I decided I wasn't going to let it affect me and I will let some strangers pull me on the floor and dance with me and let them buy a couple of drinks. I am going to have a good time. At least that is what I kept telling myself.

We make it to Sivas and park our car. Without waiting on the guys, we go on and head inside. The music is loud, and it is dark other than the strobe lights from the dance floor and the ones around the bars. Stevie, Victoria and I make our way over to the bar while Raven and her friends go out on the dance floor and start dancing. I never saw the guys come in, but I was

sure they were around here somewhere looking for the rest of us.

The bartender came over to us he had icy blue eyes and jet-black shaggy hair. He wore a V-neck white band T-shirt and dark ripped blue jeans. He asked us, "what's our choice of poison would be for the night?"

"I think we're all going to get your largest margaritas that you can make." I lean in and say to him.

"You ladies out for a girl's night?" He asked as he started on our drinks.

"Yeah! It is kind of a much-needed night." Stevie says over the loud music.

"Well ladies my name is Daven, and I will be happy to take care of such beauty all night." He gave us a very flirtatious smile as he hands us each a drink. "This round is on me."

"Well thank you Daven, definitely look forward to you making us more of these amazing drinks." I responded as I started on my drink.

We sat and drank as we talked and watched Raven and her friends on the dance floor. I spot Gabriel making his way over to them and showing off his dance moves. Without noticing James comes up beside me.

"Well, this was not what I expected when I said I wanted to talk to you," He leans on the bar, "I do apologize for everything, for what happened at school and for what the thing that wasn't me did. I am so truly sorry"

"James. Chill you can't help what happened when you got enchanted but the other parts, yeah it was all you." I took another sip of my drink.

"Yes, well, Chester told me how that thing forced himself on you and how he acted. If I had behaved better at the school, then I would have never been used in such a way or well not me but… ah you know what I mean." He shook his head and drank his beer.

"You're handling all this well… the whole finding out the magick realm is real." I sipped at my margarita and caught Daven glancing our way as if to make sure I was okay.

"Yeah, it was a shock to me at first but now it's not that shocking. By the way you look absolutely gorgeous." He leans in closer to me.

I back up slightly, "oh… well, thank you James." I look away and finish off my drink. "Daven!"

"Hey there beautiful, are you ready for another drink?" He comes over and tosses a rag over his broad shoulders.

"Yes! Please, just keep them coming." I give him a flirtatious smile and lean in a little bit on the bar.

"Anything for you beautiful." He smiles and starts on my drink.
"Stella, I'm not meaning to make you feel uncomfortable. I really do miss you…" James says to me after Daven walked away.

I cut him off, "James… please I can't do this right now I really can't. I don't feel the same way… I…"
Daven cuts in, "here you go. Is this guy bothering you?" He nods at James.
"No, it's fine Daven. Thank you." I take my drink and take a big gulp.
"Well, if you need me, I'll be here all night." He walks away to wait on someone else.
I watch him walk away and not going to lie I did check out his ass and here is where my train of thought gets interrupted again by James.
"Stella, Stella?"

"Oh, um, what?" I shake my head and revert by attention back to him.
"Did you hear anything that I said?" He asked me.
"No. Sorry I was distracted by Daven's amazing ass." I took another big gulp of my drink and avoided eye contact.
"Really?" He shook his head and fished off another beer.
"Hey, I am single so I can check out the sexy bartender if I want." I lick my lips slightly tipsy.

Chester comes running up to us. "Guys," he said in a low voice, "I don't mean to alarm anyone but there are night walkers here and they're looking for their next meal. I did some digging on this place and it turns out people come her to get fed on in hopes at becoming a night walker. They even have rooms in the back people pay extra for…. Let's just say more than feeding happens."
We all looked at him in shock. That feeling of being tipsy was short lived.
"Wait… what? So, a lot of these humans already know about the magick realm and they're not freaking out?" Victoria asked.
"Turns out with all these big-time fantasy books that everyone loves makes the humans want to be a part of it and live out their own ve their favorite books, shows, movies whatever." He shrugged. "T' is about to start, and they have that on the top floor."

Chapter 7

"We need to go up there." I said to everyone.
"Are you crazy? Once you go up there that means you are offering yourself to be feed on." Gabriel said in shock.
"It's not that big of a deal I've had it done before." I role my eyes.
"You what?" Sebastian asked in shock.

"Oh, don't get all excited we was broken up and you basically pulled another one of your vanishing acts so I went out on the weekends and would party and some just happened to be night walkers. It was actually pretty fun." I say in a rather smart tone of voice that he did not care for too much.
"We breakup and your idea of fun is to party with night walkers? You've lost your damn mind." He scolds me.
"Not all of them are bad. Some of them don't want to be a part of this war they just want to keep things as is. I might know some of them up there and if I do, we will have ears and eyes on the inside that would help us. They just want peace." I defend.
"She is right, it would help us out more if we can make peace with those that do want to keep things how they are and not wanting this war. If we join and show them that we want to help, then they will be more prone to work with us to help stop the evil that is already at our doorsteps." Chester chimes in rubbing his chin as he thought about it.
"That is true. We have to take this chance." Stevie says.
"ven." I call to the bartender. "Do you need us to pay you now or when
me down from having fun upstairs." I give him a flirty smile.
an catch me on the way out. I will keep your tab open. Go have fun."
s at us as he cleaned glasses and puts them away.

ll have to go up there. Raven you and your friends stay down

57

here and be on the lookout for anything that could go wrong, and Gabriel stay with them to protect them. James you and Sebastian should probably stay down here with them to keep them on track to stay out of trouble and to look for trouble if something was to go wrong. Keep your phones on and near you." Chester lays out the plane. "Everyone on board?"

"Yes sir." Rave salutes and downs her drink as she dragged Gabriel behind her on to the dance floor, "come on babe and dance with me." None of us even questioning the lack of any of us being 21 and at a club drinking. Fake ID's help with that.

"Let's do this." Victoria says with a smile.

I lead the way upstairs to where a group of people was sitting around but most was on the dance floor. We split up to cover more ground and as I was walking around, I heard a voice I hadn't heard in a few weeks call out to me.

"Stella!" I turn and see who was calling my name. It was a tall man with brown hair and bright green eyes. He had on a basic olive-green shirt with jeans that complimented his tan skin. He comes over to me smiling from ear to ear and in his British accent he started asking me questions excitedly.

"What are you doing here? I haven't seen you in a couple of weeks. I have missed seeing you around!"

I laugh, "Mark!" I hug him, "sorry, school got so busy!" He kissed my cheeks and gave me a tight hug.

"Ah yes I understand that I'm glad to be done with school." Mark responds. "Can I get you a drink?"

"Of course." I smile and follow him to the bar.

"You know you still have the best tasting blood I have ever had the pleasure of drinking." He eyes my neck.

"Awe, Mark, you flatter me. I know you say that to all the little witches that come around here." I joke back.

He laughs, "oh no, yours is definitely better."

"Well, you will have to have another taste while I am here. I have missed the high from it after the fact." I start having flashbacks of all the weekends spent at the different clubs enjoying the feeding frenzy with Mark and the other night walkers. Mark came home with me a lot of those nights or just come over randomly during the week and we would mess around, and he'd feed on me at the same time. He was supposed to have come over the night things got too crazy, but I canceled on him because of James. I shouldn't

58

have canceled on him and us just do our normal night of kinky sex and him feeding on me.

"Stella?" I shook my head and came out of my thoughts and realizing I was getting aroused by my thoughts of him, and my blood was pulsating hard through me, and he could tell.

"I'm fine just thinking." I took a sip of my drink. "Now how about that feeding?" I move my hair out of the way and let him sink his teeth into my skin. I let out a moan as he starts to drink my blood. I get aroused and think about him and me in my room and every dirty thing he has done to me, and I start to feel my knees go week and as I feel wetness between my legs. He leads us to a private room and pushes me up against the wall and I bring his mouth to my chest as he sinks his teeth in. I unbutton his pants and pull out his shaft. He picks me up and noticed I didn't have on any knickers. He pulls his mouth away and smirks.

"You are so naughty," He sits me down and get on his knees as his mouth kisses up my thighs and his tongue find its way between my legs. I moan and keep myself held up until he picks me back up and his large thick shaft is slid into me and starts to thrust hard and fast into me. The music is loud, so I let out loud moans as he thrust in and out me. He makes our moment quick but mind blowing. He sits me back down gently and we both try to catch our breath.

"We have got to stop meeting like this." I laugh between breaths.

"I blame you." He jokes as he fixed himself back.

I clean myself up and try to make myself look like I didn't just have a quicky in a club. Again. "Mark, we need your help. This war... It is bad. We need someone on the inside to help us. We just lost a lot of good people when we were attacked earlier today"

A grim look comes across his perfectly chiseled face. "I heard about that. I prayed you wasn't involved in it and that you haven't been killed. I will help you and I have others who want to help as well. This blood shed is senseless. Here let me heal those bite marks." He licked the side on my neck and my chest sending shivers down my spine.

"Watch it or you'll start up something else." I teased.

We leave the little room and go to find the others. I spot them at the bar upstairs observing everyone.

"Hey, so this is Mark. He is someone I have become close to during my time coming to clubs like these and he is a night walker. He wants to help."

I explained as I introduced him to the few others that was sitting at the bar. He held out his hand for them to shake it with each of them introducing themselves.

"Stella has informed me on a lot of the troubles at hand. There is a great number of night walkers that don't want this war. We have no need for it. We have places like this that allow us to enjoy feeding without killing. People know about us, and they come here because they want us to feed on them. They get a high from it. Kind of like when people smoke weed, they get the same feeling, and it won't show up if they have to do a drug test for work." He explained.

"Then why are there others that want this war?" Victoria asked.

He sighed, "some are just doing this because they're scared of the person trying to destroy everything and everyone. It has nothing to do with that they agree with wanting more power they just want to live. Then there is some that don't like having to live by the darkness. Not everyone has a piece of charmed jewelry to protect them from the sun like Stella made me a year ago." He showed his earing and the ring on his finger. "She made two for extra protection. Some was lucky and when they were changed, they didn't suffer with having what we call the vampire effect. We catch fire in the sunlight for those that are unfortunate enough to not have the ability to resist the sun." Mark looked at his hands sadly.

"Why don't we find the others downstairs and we can all come up with a plan?" Stevie asked. She changed the subject. I think she could tell it was upsetting to him.

"Good idea." Chester responded as he got up from his place at the bar and led the way down.

"So, I want every little detail on your relationship with Mark because I can tell you left something big out." Stevie whispered and Victoria nodded in agreement.

"Fine, but not here. Back at the house in your room." I whispered back.

I looked over and I saw Mark give a sly smirk my way and I knew he heard what they wanted to know.

Chester sent a text to the others to meet us outside as we made our way out of the door.

"I'm going to pay Daven then go to the bathroom." I go back over to Daven and pay him. I get my receipt and notice he had written his number down for me. I smile up at him and head to the bathroom. "Be expecting a text

from me." I gave him a wink and a little laugh.

"Stella?" I hear a familiar voice and my heart stops.

I look up and see Sebastian, "hey, I'm just going to the bathroom, but the others are already outside." I try to push past him, but he takes my arm and turns me around and pulls me into his arm. I avoid his eyes, but he tilts my chin up.

"Stella..." He pulls me closer to him and he holds me there.

I felt myself unable to speak because after everything he had said and now this.

"Sebastian... I should get back to the girls." I try to pull away, but he held me firmly in his arms.

"Stella... I don't know what to say. I'm an idiot." He kept looking at me with his perfect blue eyes.

Before I could say anything, he leans in and kisses me. I feel myself let go into his arms and his hand move down my back and grab my ass with one hand and wrapped his hand in my hair holding the back of my head as he kissed me. I felt like my head was spinning and I was short on breathing. He slowly pulls away and places his forehead on mine.

"No matter what I do I cannot quit you." His voice was raspy as he spoke to me.

"Why?" I whispered back to him placing my hands on his chest.

"Because... because... I love you..." Sebastian blurted out.

My heart skips a beat and as he spoke those words, "what?" I pull back in shock because that was the first time, he has ever said that to me in all our years of this on again off again relationship that we have.

"I love you Stella... I always have. I have just been scared to say it or admit to myself that I do. You know stupid younger me wanted to be single even though I knew I was in love with you. I just could never find the words to say it to you or courage." He looks deep into my eyes as he spoke. "I hope I can convince you to love me or fall back in love with me."

"I know no matter what I will always go back to you... and Sebastian I never stopped loving you. I have always loved you and I always will. I have never been able to be in love with anyone else or move on because I can never get past you or get over my feelings for you." I said to him.

He moved his hands to mine and brought them to his lips. My fingers tingled at the touch of his warm lips, and it sent shivers down my spine. I bite my lower lip at feeling his touch and longed for him.

"I want you, Stella. Not just for right now, I want you, all of you, now and forever. I can't see myself with anyone else and I don't want anyone else. I know that there is this crazy war going on and what the outcome could be, but I cannot walk away from you without telling you how I really feel and what I know that I have always wanted, and I want you till I take my last dying breath."

"Do you really mean it Sebastian?" I could feel my skin burning hot under his gaze as I took in every word he said.

"Yes Stella. I need you and I want you now and forever. I've been foolish all these years." He said as he looked down seeming embarrassed.

I move a hand to his face stroking his cheek, "I'll be right back, okay? I'm going to go freshen up and then we will go back to the bar."

October 22, 2021

"I excuse myself to the bathroom and that is where we are at with being caught up on everything that has been going on for this very late audio journal entry." I said as I spoke into my tape recorder at that time. I don't know why I like to do my journals like that, but I do, and I guess it is just easier. I pressed stop and made my way out of the bathroom and found Sebastian again waiting for me leaned up against the wall. "Hey, ready to go?" I asked as he took my hand.

"Yeah, let's go." He leads the way outside back to where Stevie and Victoria were at talking to James. They see us come up and the girls smiled, and I could tell they wanted to know everything once the guys weren't around, but James's expression wasn't as kind. In fact, it was cold.

"Well, I was starting to think I would have to send out a search party, but it looks like that wouldn't have been necessary." Stevie said with a smile on her face. She pulled me a little off to the side with Victoria and whispered, "okay, so what happened? Just a few hours ago you guys had split and then this Mark guy and now? Spill it girl." So, I brought them up to speed on what had happened and what all he had said. "Oh shit, just like that he broke down and finally after all the years of on again and off again he finally admitted how he felt? Damn that boy has shitty timing. He finally realizes this while we're at war. He is so smart but honey he is a dumbass all at the same damn time. Oh, and how could you not tell us about Mark? We are very insulted."

"Sorry, I just didn't know how to tell you." I smile at her reaction.

"You guys are like for real back together?" Asked Victoria.

"Yes, we are... I think?" I respond to them with a heavy sigh.

"Okay, just making sure. You might want to go let that girl that just came up to him know it as well because it looks like she is laying it on thick and she is not taking the hint he isn't interested." Victoria pointed out to me.

I look and this little blonde bombshell in a short red leather dress and red stilettos is all over Sebastian and he keeps removing her hands off him. I felt myself start getting angry and my fingers tingle with power from my emotions. I storm over there making myself known, "excuse me is there a problem here?"

The blonde bimbo looks me up and down and gives me a smartass look, "no, I'm just getting to know this sexy guy here. What do you want tubby?" She insulted back. I know I am not skinny or built very well but body shaming was not called for. I am just as surprised that I have had the attractive boyfriends that I have had and well currently have. Well, that is if Sebastian and I are back together.

"I want you to step away from my boyfriend." I cross my arms over my chest keeping a look of confidence that I really did not feel that I had. She was hot and next to her I felt like a sack of potatoes.

She scoffs out a laugh, "him, with someone like you? Ha that's funny. He is way too hot to be with someone like you."

"Okay, hold up. First off, she is my girlfriend and the love of my life so like I said before; now take your hands off me and go away. Secondly, she is the most beautiful girl I have ever seen in my life." Sebastian spoke up putting that little bimbo in her place and causing me to blush.

"You can't be for real. She is a bit of a chubby girl. She's not skinny." I started to feel self-conscious about myself even more. I knew I wasn't as skinny as I was when him and I first met but I didn't think much on it before until now. Standing next to him I do feel out of place. He is beautiful and as for me I am a lot curvier. Looking at the perfect figure on the blonde girl I was fat.

"Look, to me she is as perfect and beautiful since the first day we met. You're not going to win this, and I am not interested in some stuck-up bitch who clearly likes to come on to any and every guy thinking that her looks will get her what or whom she wants. Go find someone else that you can whore around with but leave me the fuck alone." Sebastian pulled me into him and kissed me as the girl stormed off pissed. It was not like Sebastian to go off on someone in that way. He was one for being well mannered and polite, but it seemed she had pissed him off enough that he lost his cool,

calm and collected self.

Mark claps his hands, "good job. I hate thirsty girls like that and I'm a night walker. I wouldn't even touch her neck."

Mark and I have an odd relationship. We never get jealous over each other but when we're both single we use each other for sex and fun. He knows all about my relationship with Sebastian and James and I know all about his relationships that he has been through. Okay, so yeah, he is my friend with benefit and if we're being honest, he is the best in bed. I cannot compare him to Sebastian because we have never had sex. I totally feel like a slut at this point but in my defense Sebastian and I was broken up... we never really got back together it was just speculation.

"Wait, who is this guy." Sebastian nodding over to Mark.

"I am Mark, a close friend to Stella." He holds his hand out to shake Sebastian's, but Sebastian doesn't take it he just gives him a dirty look.

"Close friends huh? She never brought you up to me." He said coldly.

"Oh really? She talked plenty about you and all the times you broke her heart." Mark smiled a friendly smile, but it was clear behind it he was ready to rip into Sebastian if he tried anything.

"Okay, I think there is enough talk on that. Down to the more important things on how the night walkers will help us stop the darkness that is coming." Stevie stepped in and spoke.

"Darkness? The night walkers live in the darkness so why would they help?" Sebastian asked ignoring Mark to try and keep his cool calm demeanor that he has always carried himself with. Feeling his phone go off he looked at the message and furrowed his brow. "The immortals are heading back. They must have found something."

"I live in the daylight and night. Stella enchanted pieces of jewelry to help me be able to walk among the living. There are others like me that is lucky to have such items to help us live like normal humans and blend in." Mark said with a smile on his face. "She got the idea from one of her favorite shows. Which I love the show as well and the little town it was filmed in is to die for. Just traveling to Georgia is so far." He chuckled. "Like I said. Vampire effect. It sucks. I wish I was lucky like some of the others that doesn't have to suffer from it."

"You did what? For some blood sucking demon? You've lost your everloving mind!" Sebastian went off on me. I stumble back at his words.

64

"Just give him a chance. You're trying to judge him before you even know him. He didn't even want the life of a night walker. His life was stolen from him from some lowlife. I just gave him some of his life back and to let him be able to live like a human and graduate from college." I defended myself. "Please don't get mad at Miss. Stella she truly has a heart of gold. I am forever thankful for her and the life she has gave back to me and everything else." Mark said with a humble voice.

"We're not done with this conversation Stella." Sebastian said coldly.

I looked down at my feet feeling like a child that just got in trouble.

"Hey, lay off of her." Mark says in a sharp voice, "hell if you would have treated her better and had not taken so long to decide what you wanted then her and I probably would have never become friends, but we have and are friends whether you like it or not." He stepped up to him with his bright lime green eyes changing to a gold color.

"Look, Sebastian. Mark is right so let's push past this because we have way more important things to take care of. Not even kidding. You know as well as I do that, we need the night walkers. So put your bruised ego aside and play nice. Hell, you both have been broke up so it should not matter what she did in your time apart." Chester said getting annoyed. "Mark, how many of you are willing to risk helping us? Sebastian how far is Argon? Did he hint as to what he found?"

"He will be at Stevie's house by the time we get there with the others. We can only hope it is good news." Sebastian held back wanting to say more but he got back to business.

"Off the top of my head I would say twenty." Mark crossed his arms and leaned up against the brick wall of the building.

Chester and the others looked at Mark shocked.

"Really? That many? I didn't expect that many. We need to head back then if Argon will be back." Chester looked between the two males that clearly did not care for one another.

"We all aren't bad despite what books, movies or shows have played us all out to be. Hell, only in the last something odd years we're now played out to be somewhat good with still showing some of us that are bad. It's only now that some are getting a few things right about us." Mark says as he sighs and runs a hand through his thick brown hair.

"I know I am the only human non magical person here, but can I just add in the walls have ears and if things are getting as bad as all you say they are

might it not be best if you all take this discussion somewhere else?" James steps in making a very good point. Never thought I would say that again.

"Mr. Kirkwood is right. We really should get out of here before we say anything else and um Sebastian, you're going to have to try getting along with the night walkers for us to not all end up dead. Enough people have died today or well now yesterday. We will work best in numbers." Raven spoke up from where she stood with her friends.

"So, it is settled. We will continue this conversation at my house." Stevie says as she leads the way to the parking lot where we parked.

"I don't know where that is." Mark responds as he follows us.

"Stella can ride with you to show you the way. You can stop along the way to get a few of your friends that want to help fight this and while you're doing that, I will address the council that is at my house and inform them on everything that we have learned so far." Stevie addresses as she unlocks her car. "We may need to contact the royal families as well. They should know what we have learned. I would say they have learned of the deaths by now."

"Wait…" Sebastian tries to speak.

"Don't start Sebastian. We must get this done so set aside your bruised ego and let this shit go. We have real problems going on." Stevie cuts him off before he can say anything else. "Call your sister so she can tell Wesley what is going on. Maybe they can come and meet with everyone. Wesley can be the eyes and ears for the royals."

I follow Mark to his ruby red Cobra that I hadn't been in, in a few weeks. He opens the door for me like always and closes it as I get in and get buckled up. He gets in on the driver side and cranks his car.

"By the way," he pulls out a pair of my lace panties to hand to me, "you left these in here."

I laugh and take them from him, "you could have just kept them as something to remember me by." I rolled my eyes as I teased him tucking them in my clutch.

He smirked and put the car in drive. "Might have to now that it seems Sebastian is determined to try and make the relationship work this time and it is not so one sided." Mark snatched my panties back and stuck them back in his glove compartment.

"Awe are you getting jealous," knowing good and well he wasn't.

He laughed and shook his head, "well, he better not screws it up once again. I'd hate to have to kick his ass but if he did it would work out for me." He winks and I shove him playfully. He takes my hand and brings it to his lips and kissed it, "I am grateful to have you Miss. Stella. You have awakened my soul more than I could have ever imagine it could be alive or dead well in my case undead."

"I'm thankful to have you in my life also and don't you worry your sexy little self. More than likely after finding out about being friends with night walkers and taking part in the feedings I have a good feeling I am about to get dumped..." I sigh, "again." I stay holding his hand and shake my head. "I just don't get it. He goes off and lived his life doing whatever the hell he wants and traveling... I mean I know it was for a good reason to seal away demons and such but when I go out and live mine and do whatever I want that makes me happy he gets pissed. It is like he expected me to just sit and wait around on him to grow up and finally want to be serious and return the same feelings that I had for him but as soon as trouble and hard times start, he loses his cool and is ready to bolt. Like what the fuck!"

"Oh Stella, you can do much better than him. I know he is the one meant to save us all because he is the only one able to seal them away unless we can find Merlin. I know he has a lot of pressure on him, and I know that many want him dead. I can see where his trust in my kind lacks. I hate there is so much evil between all the magick kind. The humans truly do not understand how dangerous our world is. Do give him a little bit of slack because he must be scared and stressed at how much he is having to take on. I never thought I would defend him, but I do know for us to stop this we do need him. He is more powerful than I think he even realizes." He squeezed my hand and looks over at me. His bright green eyes shining in the light from the streetlights as we drove to his house where two of his flat mates live.

He parks his Cobra, and he comes to my side of the car and opens my door to let me out and takes my hand.
"Why thank you kind sir." I smile up at him.
"But of course, beautiful. You deserve to be treated as a queen," the whispers in my ear, "unless in the bedroom." I get cold chills and give a flirty smile. He leads the way into his home and calls out to his friends to come into the living room. The two of them come and sit down and listen as Mark explains what is going on. They all agree to come with us because they want this ill feud to end. "I need to get a few things from my room and the rest of you should as well if you have anything that can help or to hold you over till, we can make it back here. Stella." I go with him up to his

room that I was very familiar with. I walk in and go to sit on his bed as he closed the door behind him. He slowly walks over to me.

I pull him on top of me before he could object, "drink." His eyes turn and his fangs dig into my skin. I let out a moan and hold his head to my neck as he pulled me to him. His hand starts to travel up my thigh and under my dress as we lay on his bed. I felt his hard erection pressed against me and moved my hand to unbutton his pants.

"Are you sure?" He asked me as he pulled away from my neck as my blood dripped from his mouth on to me.

"Yes." I looked up into his eyes that was searching my face.

"I don't want you to regret this later." He touched my face gently.

"I never regret anything with you." I whispered to him as I kept moving my hands to take off his pants.

"Stella…" He whispered my name and it sent chills down my spine. His lips found mine as he pulled me into him. His hands found their way down my back and to my hips, exploring my body. He slowly lifted my dress up and the feel of his fingertips electrified my skin setting my insides ablaze. Everything about this was wrong but it felt extremely right as we worked at undressing each other and before long his strong muscular body was undressed before me.

He pinned me down and planted kisses from my neck and down my chest stopping long enough to tease my nipples before moving down my stomach to my thighs before finding his way between my legs and lingered there. At this point the cold chills felt like they were not going away, and I groaned from the feel of his lips and the way he let his fangs graze my skin eager for him to skin them deep into my skin again while we had sex.

"What do you want first?" He teased as he slid three fingers into my private feeling how wet I was becoming under the power of his touch.

"Bite me and then ride me harder than you ever have before," I begged. He wasted no time as his eye turned hungry and sunk his fangs deep in my neck and then my breast drinking from me as he held me down and drove his member hard and slow in and out of me savoring the moment as I let myself be consumed by him. I felt myself throbbing around him as the climax builds. I don't hold back as I moan loudly as we make the bed squeak and the headboard hit the wall. I know his flat mates can hear us, but I don't care. I only care about what Mark is doing to me and how it makes me feel right in this moment. They've heard us before I am sure of it, and it won't be the last time either.

Mark pulls his mouth from one of my breasts as blood drips from his fangs and mouth on to my naked body. The sight turns me on as I see him lick his lips and eyeing where he will feed from me next. "Let me lick my blood off your fingers." He does as I ask, and he groans.

"Do you enjoy the taste of blood? Or being railed by a demon?" He asked. "I know the answer to that but feel free to answer me anyways you dirty girl." He teased me.

"Hum, maybe just a little." I lick my lips and felt his hand wrap around my neck squeezing it taking and cutting of my air. I closed my eyes and felt him pin both my wrist above my head with his free hand and he went back to sinking his fangs into the open place between my neck and shoulder. I gasp and he squeezed my neck a little more and it only made me want more.

He rode me hard, and I felt him starting to pulsate in me. "You're so tight. I feel you throbbing around me. I don't know how much longer I can last." He starts going harder and harder and I can't hold myself back any longer as I feel myself explode around him and him in me. He collapses on top of me panting hard.

"Maybe we should get going before they send out a search party for us." I suggest in a shaky voice as I worked to calm myself down. I honestly did not want it to end. I wanted him to keep going till I could not walk anymore, leaving my legs shaking like he had done before.

"True, let me clean up your bite marks." He offered as he went through and made them vanish while he licked them up.

We got up and started to get dressed, "you might want to pack a small bag or something," I told him.

He grabbed a bag and started to gathered things into it for the rode. "Not a bad idea. We wouldn't want to have to sneak back here for some more fun." He winked at me. "Maybe next time we won't have to be in such a hurry and can really get kinky."

"Such a tempting offer." I walk over to him and run my hand up his chest. "You know how much I love when things get kinky in the bedroom."

"Just in the bedroom." He raised an eyebrow and smirked.

"Okay, not just the bedroom." I start to think about all the places we had snuck off and had a little fun and start to get turned on again, "we really need to go before I take your clothes off again."

We laugh and leave his bedroom and find his friends downstairs playing video games in their living-room that they had set up with three TVs hooked

up for gaming. "Ready to go?" They looked up and nodded as they logged off.

"Question is are you both ready?" Jay smirks as he looked between us.

"Oh, shut up." I replied and head, out the door and to Mark's Cobra to make our way to Stevie's house.

He backs his car out of the driveway and throw it into drive and speed towards Stevie's house. "Tell me where to go."

I gave him a rundown of where to go and he quickly drove us there. Fifteen minutes later we made it to her house with gravel flying.

Mark comes to my side of the car to let me out and then we moved the seat up so his friends could get out. "Come on, everyone should be here." I lead the way up the walk and into the house, "Stevie! Victoria! We made it."

They come around the corner from the study.

"Stella! Did you bring some of his friends?" Victoria asked.

"Yes, this is Jay and Skyler. They're Mark's flat mates." They held out their hands to Stevie and Victoria.

"Nice to meet you guys. Mark here tells us that there are others like the three of you that want to fight on our side and put an end to this evil." Stevie says.

"Yes, we honestly don't want any fighting, but it looks like there is going to be a war and if we're going to have to fight it will be alongside you guys. Plus, Stella here is cool as fuck and if she needs our help, we're here to serve. She has helped all of us so much and when we were forced to turn against our will because of some bitchy night walker she made us these sun light protection things out of jewelry we have." Jay showed us his cross around his neck and Skyler showed us his ring. "We will do what we can to help and so will all the others. There is some that are for all this evil and do like to kill and drain the life out of people but then you have night walkers like us that aren't like that." Jay went on.

"Well, it is great to have you all, come on into the study. We're getting started on a new plan and with you guys now in on this we can get the show on the road." Stevie invited them into the house, so they weren't stuck standing on the porch.

"Mom, Dad, here are the night walkers we had told you about. There is more but we will get to them later." Stevie calls to them as we walk through the entrance way into the study.

Phoebe and Luke looked up from their spot at the desk with Sebastian. Sebastian and I make eye contact and I felt my heart fall into my stomach, but I didn't let it show.

"Stella! Sweetie come on over here and bring your friends." Phoebe smiles and beckons us to come over.

"Went out for a fun night of partying and came back with some friends that want to help us fight this thing that threatens to plague the human and magick realm." I half joke and walk over and give her a hug and try to avoid Sebastian's gaze. It was hard to make light of everything that was going on. Considering what also taken place and some of our friends did not make it to see daylight. It did feel wrong to joke but I really did not know what else to do other than cry and I could not just break down, but I knew one was coming from all the stress.

Sebastian clears his throat, "well, we need to go over this plan. Now who has been in and out of the enemy territory?"

"I have…" Mark spoke up, "I've had to go in plenty unfortunately."

"Then you get to be our eyes and ears. What do you know so far?" Sebastian asked.

"They're located in a warehouse on the waterfront. There is four points of entry which obviously is also the exit. The roof, two fire exits on the left wing and the right wing and then the one in the back of the building where the trailers come in at and the front entry. They always have each post guarded. The holding cells are on the third floor and the top floor is where that one young witch, is being used as a puppet." Mark explains. I can see his knuckles turn white as he explained the layout the best he could and what he got to see. "They're determined to get to you Sebastian. They honestly all think Merlin is dead."

Chapter 8

"They don't care who has to die in the process as long as they have you in the end to complete what they have planned and no turning yourself in won't do any good either. We're all dead anyways if they get their hands on you and your powers. The thing that is possessing that girl now wants your body and your powers." Mark went on.

We all looked at him.

I felt a shiver go up my spine and I looked to Sebastian who stood with his arms crossed and I could tell he had his teeth clinched from how tight his jaws looked. His perfect blue eyes looked serious and deep in thought. I wondered what he was going to do. This was worse than we ever thought it was. I know I keep saying that but really… it is… it just keeps getting worse and worse with each passing news. It wasn't just the thought of death that I could lose him to it was to total darkness that was trying to kill all that is good. That was worse than death to me… to all of us.

"Sebastian don't try to do anything to rash. You can't go at this alone and none of your friends would let you even if you tried. If you even dare, try on your own you will end up possessed or dead and then you would not be doing any of your friends and family any favors that way. You will just get us all killed." James stepped forward and spoke up after a long moment of us all being silent taking in everything Mark was telling us. I was honestly surprised at how forward he was on the matter as I looked at him taking a sip of his bourbon, he had poured himself. Something in me felt aroused by watching him and his demeanor. I quickly shook the thought out of my head for it to only linger. "Mark, is there a moment of weakness at any point during the day that would be best to attack?" James asked bringing me back from flashbacks of him and I. 'What is wrong with me? I can't still have feelings for him. Can I?' I thought to myself. 'I swear I am such a hot fucked up mess. What the hell?'

Mark searched his mind for a moment looking for the right answer, but none came to mind.

"I honestly don't know. We're night walkers, demons we don't need sleep we still doze though. We do need to feed though… They have somewhat of a shift change you could say to let everyone get to take turns to go feed. That would be the only thing I could think of that would be somewhat of an opening to attack but it isn't a big one."

"Looks like that will just have to work for us to at least try something. Do you all have something to help you move around in the daylight?" James asked.

"No, only it's trusted circle does. We only have them because of Stella. The rest aren't as lucky as we are if they don't have any friends that are witches or warlocks." Mark responded back to him showing his that protects him in the sun. "Or if you are not lucky enough to be the ones who wasn't cursed with the vampire effect. Aside from that you are fucked in the daylight without charmed jewelry."

"I think I have an idea. It's far-fetched but it might just work. What if a spell was cast that was bright and strong enough to act as the sun to kill off a lot of the night walkers?" James asked. More and more I am starting to remember why I was attracted to him so much and it just isn't helping the situation any. I could kick myself right now.

"That might actually work." Luke chimed in after listening and thinking it all over. "If we can channel each other enough to link together we can cast a strong enough spell to kill many of them. Mark I would recommend that you and your friends stay here out of harm's way. The rest of us need to get to work on spells."

"What if I enchant items for us to have on our person for protection incase things start going wrong and maybe a two way magnify spell so we can communicate with knowing if anyone of us is in trouble?" I asked.

"That would be helpful Stella, why don't you girls work on that, and the elders and Sebastian will work on the daylight spell." Luke ordered.

We all went off our separate ways to get everything ready for what was to come for tomorrow and to get some sleep because we were going to need all the sleep we could get. I left the bathroom after entering in my latest diary voice entry and ran into James. He held me by my shoulders, and I looked up at him and felt my breath leaving me.

"Stella?" I heard a voice behind me, "umm are you coming?" It was Stevie

"Y-yeah… on my way." I reluctantly pulled away from him not letting my eyes leave his. "I'll see you later…" I said breathlessly.

He gave me a look only he could and that sexy half smile that he does that makes me want to jump him right then. "Are you feeling okay Stella you look a bit…."

"Seems we missed a bit of the fun." A voice chimes in making everyone stop what they were doing and look up.

"Daniel…" Sebastian says with his eyes wide at the sight of his friend he thought was dead. Daniel, whom we had discovered was Merlin and now much to all, of our surprise he has returned.

Daniel smirked as he looked at us all. "You look as if you've seen a ghost."

Chapter 9

We stood in shock for what seemed like a good long while. He was there standing in front of us. Merlin had in fact returned.

"You think? What happened? Romeo saw you get sealed away." Sebastian went over to him. It was clear he was in disbelief but honestly how could he not be? We all were.

"Long story short. I was. Technically. I just managed to get free and keep Areses sealed away. It just took a little bit. A lot a bit." Daniel replied with a shrug and walked more into the study and looked around eyeing the books on the shelf and then Sebastian's set up on the table.

"Okay… Argon how did you find him?" Sebastian questioned with slight confusion in his voice.

Argon rubbed his chin and chuckled. "We used Amethyst. Pretty much he was like our little hound dog sniffing out for his master and we lucked up on finding the crystal and then Merlin got himself out. Which I still cannot figure out how you did that."

"Magick." Daniel replied sarcastically wiggling his fingers at the immortal who looked at him clearly not amused by the old wizard who never looked like he aged.

"No shit Sherlock." Argon grumbled and rolled his eyes and went to go lean up against the wall near the entranceway to the study. Citrine giggled at the comment and wrapped her arms around Argon resting her head on his chest. He kissed the top of her head and smiled down at her.

"Then why ask such a stupid question?" Daniel retorts and whistles like he was calling for a puppy. "Here Amethyst, here boy."

Amethyst trotted in proudly and went to sit next to his master like a proud show dog.

"Is it just me or is it really weird seeing a dragon act like a wee pup?" Chester

chimes in with a chuckle and walked over to stand with Sebastian.

"D- Daniel…" We heard a voice coming from the threshold of the hallway. It was Clara. The expression on her face broke my heart. "You came back…" Daniel looked back and his eyes widened. "Clara." He rushed over to her and without care he lifted her up and kissed her deeply. A soft sob could be heard leaving Clara's lips between the deep kisses they were sharing. "Of course, I did. I promised you that I would princess. I will always keep my promise to you."

I could only wish to know more of their past lives together. The time he served for Camelot. Maybe one day. I only learned some of it from Romeo and the immortals that was willing to talk and told me what they knew. I knew a lot of it was tragic and heart wrenching but the fact that they always found one another in each life was beautiful. I knew Merlin never actually died he would do this thing Romeo called a Phoenix Effect I took it as like the thing The Doctor does in Doctor Who, regeneration. It is sad I relate things to my favorite shows. As for Morgana she would be reborn in different lives. She would not remember anything though not until later, but Merlin would always be able to find her and be there waiting until she remembered.

"Step away from my wife." Wesley's voice speaks up coldly.

Daniel slightly pulled away from Clara to glare at Wesley. "How about no? I think I will take being tortured than leave her. I do not give a damn that she was forced to wed you. It does not change the fact that I love her, and she loves me."

Now can more men be like this? Knows what they want and will fight tooth and nail for the one they love to be with them. That is all I ask for. Is that to, much to ask for?

Clara clung to Daniel and hid her face in his chest. I am still not sure if I should be calling him Daniel or Merlin. This is confusing. Either way it was clear she was not going to leave his embrace and who could blame her. Hell, I wouldn't want to leave those arms either.

"Clara. Come here." Wesley's voice was stern, but his eyes held hurt behind them. "Please." He held his hand out for her to take it, but she wouldn't, and he lowered his hand and licked his lips and nods giving a half laugh. "Of course. He is back… but that does not change the fact you are my wife. The mother to our child that you are pregnant with." Can I say I did not see that last part coming?

"What…?" Daniel pulled away slightly and looked down at Clara who wouldn't look at him. "Clara… is this true?" She didn't answer. "It is…" he

lets out a sad shaky breath.

"Of course, it is true why would I lie about something like that?" Wesley scowls and walked in a little more. "Okay, let us just get back to business. You requested me to be here so here I am. Explain to me what all is going on over here thus far that you are aware of in the states please."

I could tell he just wanted to change the subject and get down to business.

"Yes, of course. Why don't we come back into the study and chat? If you would like the rest of you kids can go on and get to bed to get some sleep. I will catch up our young prince and Merlin here. Sebastian, will you join us?" Luke calls out to him as he went back into the study. He looked tired like he did not get enough sleep while we were gone. Honestly, we all looked wore out.

Sebastian looked sadly at his little sister. I could see the worry he had for her in his eye, "Go get some rest Clara." He said to her softly and kissed the top of her head.

Clara nods and looked back up at Daniel who looked at her sadly.

"I am sorry I took too long to come back to you." Daniel whispered to her in such a sad voice it broke my heart. It was clear he was hurt by the fact she was not only married but pregnant by another man.

I took Clara by the hand. "Hey, come on. You can come and stay with the girls and me. One big sleepover." I tried to lighten the mood, but I could tell that the life for the most part had left her eyes. That bright light she once held. It was dead. "Oh Clara…" I whispered as we walked up the stairs together.

I watched her look back at Daniel and him her.

"Goodnight, Clara… I love you." He said to her.

I watched Clara stop and look him over sadly before she replied. "I love you… more than anything." She looked back at me and followed me up the stairs. What was said after we went to Stevie's room, I am not sure. I suppose it was just all that had taken place and the plan we had come up with.

We went into Stevie's room where the other girls were sat chatting. Stevie looked up at us and she frowned at the sad looking Clara that was next to me. "Come join us. We're just getting ready to get some sleep. I have some clothes you can change in to." She got up and went over to her chest of drawers and pulled out a pair of pjs for Clara to change in to.

"Thank you." Clara replied softly as she took the clothing.

"The bathroom is just through that door, and you are welcome." Stevie nods to the bathroom.

Clara hesitated and gave a small nod and went into the bathroom closing the door behind her to get changed.

I looked at Stevie and the others. We didn't say anything. We knew the situation was sad. It felt like the past two days had blurred together and so much had happened in a blink of an eye. We did however have more hope. Merlin was back and if we were luck our enemy would be none the wiser to that and it would give us a better chance at getting a head start in this whole thing to bring them down and stop all this darkness and deaths. At least I had hope for that. That is all we could do now. Have hope. Part of me was also selfish to the fact that now Sebastian would not have to risk his life now that Merlin was back. Coming out of my thoughts I hear Clara come out of the bathroom. She looked like she had been crying silently behind closed doors. My heart broke for her.

"Okay girls. Time for lights out and to get at least a few hours of sleep." Victoria chimes in to break all our train of thoughts.

Chapter 10

The next morning felt like it came to soon but then again, I don't think we got to sleep till a little after 2 in the morning, but I could be wrong. I rolled over to look at my phone to see the time. It was 9 in the morning. I felt like I had been hit by a bus. I was tired and judging by looking around the bedroom at the other girls they were feeling the same way. I reluctantly sat up and stretched. "I could drink a whole pot of coffee." I yawned and stretched only to lay back down to close my overly tired eyes.

"Come on. We all need to get up." Stevie shakes my shoulder and I groan in response. "Any normal day I would be all for sleeping in but unfortunately we cannot." I opened one eye and watched her get out of bed.

Letting out a sigh I got up and looked around the room. "Where is Clara?" I questioned and realized she was missing.
Stevie furrowed her brows together. "I wonder if she got up early to go find Daniel?"
"Hell, I would to. Did you see him? Plus, the way he looks at her and just... just all of that. They do not make guys like that anymore." Raven chimes in as she got to her feet from where she had been sleeping on a little cot that she had made on the floor. "That kiss was so romantic." She sighs with a little smile on her face.
Stevie and I giggled as we watched her.
"You know, she has a very good point." I got up and started to dig out clothes for the day out of my bag. Mostly consisted of an oversized sweater and black ripped jeans and knee-high boots to match.
 "Well, I am pretty sure he only has eyes for one person so you both are out of luck." Stevie teased.

Making our way downstairs we made our way into Stevie's kitchen where we found a few of the others. Chester was of course eating. No surprise at all on that. I swear I would love to know where it all goes. Anyways, I looked around to see if Clara had made it to the kitchen, but I still did not see her. I frowned and poured myself a cup of coffee and added the pumpkin spice creamer. (And yes, before you ask, I am that basic white girl.) Sipping at my coffee I watched Stevie go and kiss Chester good morning. He had a mouth full of pancake but still kissed her back. He looked like a chipmunk. It was cute. They are adorable together.

"Good morning, everyone." A voice says as they walk into the kitchen. Glancing over to the voice that held an Italian accent as he spoke, I give a polite smile at Daniel and quickly realized Clara was with him hugging his arm with a light blush on her cheeks. She had a bit more life to her eyes and that made me happy. I looked them both over and looked back at Stevie. We both gave a knowing look as to what those two had been up to.

"Well, good morning to you both. So, this is where you vanished off to." I tease and give a playful wink to Clara who blushed a deeper red.

Daniel chuckled and looked down at Clara lovingly. "It was well worth getting up late." She looked up at him and gave a shy smile and he kissed her nose.

"Okay, you both are way too cute." Rave leaned on the counter with her coffee between her hands. "Now how can I get that?"

I laugh at her comment that seemed to make the others in the room give a laugh as well. It was nice. The calm... but really this was the calm before the storm. We knew this pleasant, sweet moment wasn't going to last. Much like the short-lived sleepover last night before many died. Every simple, precious moment that has been taken for granted has been catching up to me and I think to the others as well. Just for the little looks, expressions and tone of voice and even body language.

"Is Lilith still at Prospero?" I asked Clara before taking another sip of my coffee.

"Yes, mother and father have not pulled us out. It is my last year though and I will graduate in May." Clara replied to me. She wasn't leaving Daniel's side. Her arms stayed wrapped around one of his arms and he did not seem to mind it. I think it made him happy. That is until Wesley came in with Sebastian.

Wesley's expression darkened quickly. If we didn't need Merlin, I think Wesley would have killed him or had him killed. Well, at least tried to. Probably would just torture him to no end but from the looks of it and what I have heard, Merlin will gladly take it if it meant saving or protecting the woman he loves. I can only imagen everything that man had been put through in the past and even now, yet he shows no fear or regret. I have never met or seen anyone like Merlin. Yes, Sebastian is brave and noble and has always been a gentleman and has always tried to do everything by the books and be just but romantically he has always struggled with that part, but he does try. He has always pulled my chair out for me, opened my car door, picked up the tab and has never made me pay for anything, he would walk on the sidewalk that the traffic was on. He just has this old-fashioned way about him that I do love but he has continued to have trouble staying in a relationship. He lets everything else keep him from that and, I think he is just scared to be in one.

Wesley and Merlin glare at one another. You could feel the hate that the two had for one another.
Sebastian walked over to me and followed my eyes to watch and see what would happen but knowing him he would step in the middle of it to shut it down.

"Okay, why don't we go over what you guys talked about last night? Anything new?" Stevie chimes in before the two start a fight.
"Yes, Daniel made the ward around the property more stable. He fixed anything I missed on from never creating a ward as big as this on my own… anyways, Daniel plans to face whoever the puppet master is alone so none of us are pulled in and put at risk of being killed." Sebastian explained.
Clara pulled away from Daniel and looked at him with fear and shock, "you are what? Why would you do this? I… we… just got you back and now you are going to go risk your life?"
Daniel looked away and ran his fingers through his dark hair.

"Answer me…" Clara whispered in a hurt voice. "Why?" She looked over to Wesley who held no concern for Daniel's safety. He looked back coldly. It was clear he would have rather Daniel stayed gone.

"Because it has to be done. He is the only one strong enough to shut things down from the inside." I looked over to see the voice that had poke

up. It was Argon. The immortal walked in and rested his hand on Daniel's shoulder. "But we will be close by in case things do not go as plan. This is only day three since things have gotten worse, correct? And it is only going to keep being just that. A year ago, is when all hell broke loose. Things was or seemed under control, but it quickly proved us to be wrong. We did not know just what Areses, and his children did when they were free. They awoke more of the already dormant night walkers and demons. Some like Mark and his friends that had been living in the shadows in peace have been forced into helping the ones who want to only cause harm and grief. We have to think of them as well and get them out of that and save others before they become nothing more than a tool for this rising crisis."

Clara I could tell knew that Argon was right, but it didn't stop her from having a look of despair. I couldn't blame her. The love of her life just came back from basically the dead even though he wasn't killed but still.

"It isn't fair… why is it always having to be you? It has always been you always risking everything trying to save everyone." Clara said in such a soft sad voice I could hardly hear her when she spoke.

I watched Daniel look back at her and without care of the young prince being in the room he pulled Clara to him and tilted her chin up so he could look her in the eyes. His eyes and expression held so much love in them. The way he held her and spoke to her is something I had never seen before. It was a love like any other and if I had to beat money on it, it would be a love that would end all darkness and war. Only that is something you read about in fantasy and romance novels, not something in the real world. I guess I shouldn't count that out though. It is Merlin after all and from everything I have heard, he can do things that none of us can began to imagine.

"Clara, I will be alright. I have the advantage." Daniel's voice was strong and authoritative as he spoke to her, but it was also gentle. It was clear he did believe that he was going to put an end to all of this but just from looking around the room some believed it and some sadly did not. "You need not worry over me princess." He kissed her lips gently and even for me it made my own heart flutter so I know it must have hers as well and plus her cheeks turning red kind of gave it a way.

Wesley on the other hand was not thrilled about what just happen. I guess I cannot blame the guy. Another man kissing his pregnant wife does look rather bad. Even if it was an arranged marriage that Clara wanted no part of. Breaking my thought bubble, I hear Wesley speak up. "I would advise you

to let go of my wife." His look and the sound of his voice got much darker the last time he had spoken up. It seemed that within just seconds his whole demeanor changed, it got darker.

"You mean the woman you stole from me?" Daniel challenged, clearly unfazed by the darkness that was looming over the young prince.

"I did no such thing. Our marriage was arranged. Now if you will, unhand her. I am taking her back home where she will be safer and heavily guarded. She does not need to be in the middle of this where she could be at risk of getting killed or losing the child that can also risk her health." Wesley stepped forward without fear of what Daniel could do to him. He held his hand out for Clara to take it.

"Clara, Wesley is right. It will be safer for you to not be here. Mother and father is having Lilith be sent there as well away from what could be the line of fire. The ward at the school is holding up but they still fear that it won't hold if there is another attack." Sebastian had a point and so did Wesley. It would be safer that way for them both. I could tell that Clara was weighing in her thoughts on what Sebastian had just said to her plus what Wesley had said. "Please Clara, I would worry for you if you stayed." Sebastian added.

Clara frowns and looked back up at Daniel who met her curillin blues with that of his own. "As much as I do not want you to go... they are both right." Daniel spoke softly to her, "I promise I will come back to you. I always do." Clara hesitated to let him go and took Wesley's hand that he still held out to her. "You better Daniel." Was her response to him.

"You have my word my princess. I will always find my way back to you. No matter what." The way he spoke and looked at Clara showed he meant every word of it. I have never seen anything like it and judging by some of the other girls in the room they hadn't either.

Wesley rolled his eyes in response. Everyone could feel just how much the two hated one another. It was slightly unsettling. Jay steps in hesitantly and I gave him a look of worry.

"What is it, Jay?" I heard Mark questioned him and walked over to him to bring him in more.

"Th- the girl that is being used. One of the others found out by whom. It is a woman. She goes by Ophelia." Jay said nervously, "she knows Merlin is back. She wants you to come to her... revenge. Something about the past... what did you do Merlin?" He looked back at Daniel whose expression went dark.

"I see. What happened is none of your concern." Daniel replied quickly. "Get Clara out of here. Now. I have work to do."

We stood shocked watching Daniel turn on his heels to leave the kitchen. I blinked a few times working to process what just happened. "Is he really not going to tell us what the hell he did that has caused this woman to go to these links she has went? People are dying! Why is he keeping this a secret?" I demand as anger builds up in me over this. I wanted to go confront him and I started to until James grabbed my arm to stop me. I look up at him already livid. "Let me go." I said to him through gritted teeth. "You're not in any position to stop me."

"Stella. I want to know just as much as you do but going about it with this temper will not make him talk. So threatening James is not going to get you anywhere." Argon walked up and separated us. "In all my years of knowing that man I can tell you one thing. He has more secrets than any man I have ever met. He is the only person that I cannot read the mind of that I have come across. Trust me when I say this. He will not talk. He has been tortured to the point of almost death and still never talked. So not even your hot redheaded temper cannot make him talk."
I worked to calm down. I knew Argon was right. I could see it in his eyes and hear it in his voice, but it still did not change my now distrusted feelings I held for Daniel, "fine, but he better start talking. If all this happening is because of him…"
"You'll what?" Argon challenged me.
I glared up at the immortal. His dark brown eyes looking back at me with a serious gaze. "I will find a way to deal with him myself because it seems the lot of you is too scared to stand up to him."

"Do not be an idiot and so quick to judge. The ones of us that knows Merlin and know what to expect from the evil we are facing knows that we need

Merlin to be able to stop them. Merlin is lesser of those evil. He may have his secrets, but he is the only one that can stop them. Yes, we are immortals, but our powers are not equipped to handle the evil that is plaguing the planet. Even if it is all due to an old vendetta." I looked over to see a woman I had not seen before. Her skin was dark and flawless with her dark hair perfect to match falling neatly down her back. She was accompanied by a male with raven black hair pulled back out of his eyes. His skin was pale. He was attractive with high cheekbones and dark eyes. He had down pat that tall dark and handsome look. I could only assume that this was Carnelian and Agate.

"I take it you are Carnelian and Agate." I said to them.

"Oh, look she has a brain." Carnelian said to me smartly. That only made me even more mad. "Oh, did I strike a nerve? Pity." She gave me a smirk. I have never wanted to hit someone so bad before until now.

"Okay, enough you two." Argon chimes in. "Let us get along and not add to the problems we are already having to deal with. Like it or not Stella we need Merlin so calm down and Carnelian play nice."

I glared at the two of them and then looked to Clara who looked back at me. I could tell she knew something but wasn't saying anything. "Who is Ophelia?" I asked her.

Clara looked down at the hands nervously. "She was what you would call a lady in wait. She came from a noble family. We did trade with them. Their father was in the spice business. Uther was going to marry me off to her older brother, Lord Thomas. Only Thomas was murdered in his chambers one night, we never knew by whom or for the reason why. He was a good man…. But Ophelia… she… she wasn't as kind as her brother. She almost seemed jealous of him and his relations. The ways she looked when he was in the company of another woman…. It was unsettling. I always thought she killed him but there was no proof of it." Clara looked at us all and it was clear even Argon didn't know this information. "I always believed she was in love with her brother. A silly thought really."

"Or Merlin killed him out of jealously." Wesley chimes in from where he stood with his arms crossed over his chest.

Clara shot him a look, "Merlin would never do that. He was loyal to the crown and the nobles."

"But he is more loyal to you and making sure you stay his. No matter the cost." Wesley retorts. "I do not have to read his mind to know that he will kill me as soon as he gets the chance. Now let us get you home."

Clara looked at Wesley in shock. But the young prince had a point. I was starting to not trust Merlin. I knew Sebastian trusted him. Even Jenna and Sally and of course Chester. Something about him made me wonder if we ever fully could trust him. The number of secrets he held; it was unsettling to me. Was he really the only person left we could count on? Was what we were facing really the enemy that we should all fear? Or was it the man in the study that everyone was so worried about getting back to save us all? I made up my mind. I did not trust him. I couldn't.

Chapter 12

October 23, 2021

It was a new day. Everyone was still on edge from yesterday. Clara was sent back to Wesley's kingdom where Lilith was waiting for her. From what I had been told and heard Lilith was scared and shaking when Clara arrived. The school had been targeted when the little girl was leaving and some of the students was hurt. She was shaken. Who could blame her? We got word that the school took another hit this morning. Daniel thinks they are going after his mother and Romeo and then will hit the palace next to go after Clara and Lilith. He is working over his next move. Things will be changing in the plan. It seems he is planning to go back to Prospero. Back to the school. Back where this darkness first started for us but not where it started for him.

"Hey Stella! Are you coming down?" A voice called up from the stairs pulling me away from my train of thought while I did my journal voice entry. I knew it was Stevie.
"Yeah, I'm coming!" I call back. "And sa…"
"Do you always talk to yourself?" I turned around surprised. I didn't hear him or know I was being watched.
"Agate… oh… this is just how I do my journal entries. I talk into this tape recorder. Each tape after it is full, I store away after I label it with the month, days and year." I explained to him. His raven black hair fell in front of his dark eyes. He was very much attractive and had a dominating aura about him. Agate never took his eyes off me and part of that made me blush and draw back.
"Interesting. Do all mortals do this now?" He questioned me. His thick British accent rolled off his tongue smoothly as if it was coated in honey.

88

I shook my head and stepped back from him slightly, "no. Many still wright it all down. I like it this way… plus I can leave it on to record if I wish."

"Is that so? Is it recording now?" Agate questioned stepping closer to me. My breath hitched in my throat as I stumbled back, and he caught me. "Watch your step." He took the tape recorder from my hand and looked it over and watched the blinking red light. "So, you are recording our conversation." He smirked as he still held me to him and looked back down into my green optics with his dark ones.

I blushed a deep shade of read as if the finding out and getting caught was embarrassing. It slightly was. Very few know of my odd little quirk and now someone I hardly know does and it added on to my self-consciousness. "Can you let me go now?" I asked in a whisper. I could hardly hear myself, but he heard me and let me go stepping away from me and returning my tape recorder back to me. I hugged it to my chest and looked up at him. "Thank you." Turning on my heels I ran quickly down the hall to avoid lingering around him any longer. It felt like my heart was going to pound out of my chest.

Reaching the stairs, I gripped the railing I took a moment to catch my breath and compose myself. Tucking away the tape recorder in my jacket pocket I let out a heavy sigh and started down the stairs, replying what just happened in my head I tripped on the last step and let out a startled scream before I face planted the floor, I felt someone catch me. (I really must stop being so damn clumsy. Like what the hell?) Looking up I met with dark brown eyes that held amusement.

"So, I see you're still just as graceful as ever." The voice said to me.

"Jenna!" I recovered and quickly pulled her in and hugged her. "Is Sally here with you?" I asked and pulled away slightly. She was still just as beautiful as the last time I saw her. She had cut her hair short, and she had a boyish look to her that made my heart flutter. Can't lie, she could turn any girl. I could easily go from Bi to lesbian in a heartbeat. "And can I just say… Damn. Did you get hotter in a year?"

Jenna gave a laugh and ran her fingers through her hair and bit her lower lip and gave a shrug. Her arms now held sleeved tattoos and she had snake bite piercings and her nose pierced and smaller gages and her left eyebrow pierced. She had the look of someone you wanted to make all the wrong decisions with. "First off, you completely ignored what I said to you. Secondly, I will talk about that here soon with everyone and thirdly, thank you. Now come on. I have news too share."

I furrowed my brow. I noticed her demeanor had changed and my gut feeling was telling me something was wrong even though Jenna hid her feelings, but it was clear whatever it was, wasn't good.

"Jenna! You came." Chester moved to her quickly to pull her in and hugged her tightly. "Where is Sally?"

Jenna squeaked out her breath and pulled away from the bear hug. "Down Chester…" She coughed out. "I am sorry it took so long to get here. Ran into some trouble while out on a dig… Sally was killed."

All our hearts dropped.

"What?" Chester breathed out and looked back at Stevie who held the same heartbreaking look from the news.

"We were attacked. A lot of us on the job site didn' make it. Fifty of us went out and only ten of us made it back and that wasn' with lack of tryin' to save the others. Sally went back to try and save one of the men that was being pulled back into the cave by these things. They were ripping him apart." Jenna was shaking. We could all tell she was trying to hold it together, but the loss of her girlfriend was weighing on her. "Before I could even get to her… they tore her apart… they ripped her and all of them apart like they were nothing but rag dolls."

"Oh Jenna… I am so sorry." I managed to get out as tears ran down my face. I couldn't believe it. Sally was murdered.

"Where was this at?" A voice spoke up. Looking back, I saw it was Daniel. His blue eyes were cold and serious. I didn't trust him. Not anymore at least.

Jenna swallowed hard. "Our excavation site was in the ruins of Angkor, Cambodia. We had discovered a hidden cave under the old ruins of the city when one of the streets had collapsed after a storm. We used our gear for climbing and went down in teams to set up lights and the equipment and started to explore what we had found. One team stayed back, and the rest of use followed our boss. We didn't know we would stumble across a den."

How she was able to hold it together was beyond me but if I had to guess, it was for the sake of revenge. To avenge Sally and the crew she worked with. Watching Daniel, he narrowed his eyes and rubbed his chin. "A den?" I could tell his wheels was turning in his head. Even for someone as old as him it seemed he was even shocked at that news. "What did those creatures

90

look like. Can you draw them out for me?" Daniel held out a notebook and a pen to her for her to take.

Jenna looked at the notebook and pen then back at Daniel. "Yes. Of course." She took them from him and sat at the table, "do you think they are related to what has been going on?"

"I am not sure yet. What I do know is, we must stop this from continuing. This could be an entirely different threat that we are facing, or they are some of Ophelia's sick creations." Daniel replied and walked over to the window to look out over the colorful fall foliage that painted the woods around the house. I watched as his brow furrows. "We are being watched."

"Yes, Callen and some of the other elves are keeping watch from the property line. He said some of the enemies are trying to break through." Argon chimes in and walked over to where Daniel was and ran his eyes along the property line.

"I feared as much. We need to act quickly. The school was attacked again. I do not know how much longer its defenses can last." Daniel looked back to see Jenna finishing the picture she had sketched out on the notebook. He walked back over to her and looked over her shoulder. His eyes went dark, and he sucked on the front of his teeth. "It seems we have more than one problem on our hands. I am sorry, allow me to handle the current problem and then I will help you and you will get your revenge. You have my word."

Jenna gave him a nod. "Of course. They would want this issue resolved first. To save everyone else." She looked back at the others; her brown eyes held a mix of emotion, but it was mostly determination.

Raven rushed in with her two friends. They both looked horrified. "The ward is crumbling at the school!" All three of them said at the same time.

Chapter 13

News that we didn't want to hear. The room went silent in shock. It seemed that the enemy wasn't going to let up on their attacks and to make it worse they were now attacking the castle where Clara and Lilith were. It was no secret what they were trying to do. They wanted to force Daniel out and make him decide the fates of those being targeted. No matter what many was going to die and not even Merlin could be in two places at once. At least I thought so.

"Merlin you cannot be serious? You are really going to send this doll version of yourself to the school so you can go to the castle?" Argon argued and pointed to a little clay doll that was laid out on the table.

"Yep." Daniel quips back without looking at the immortal. "Now where is that spell for this? It has been some time since I last used it." He murmured to himself and flipped through the pages of an old leather back book. Argon looked to the other immortals for help on this. The look on his face showed he was at a loss. Agate held up his hands showing he was staying out of it. Citrine giggled and placed a gentle hand on Argon's shoulder. "Let him do this. We must have faith. You and I will accompany the real Merlin to the castle and Agate and Carnelian can go with the puppet. We can even have doubles of ourselves as well. It could help throw them off more. One of Sebastian as well. They will not be able to know which is the real ones of us." She said to her lover.

Argon looked down into her green eyes then to his companions before letting out a heavy sigh. "Okay. You have a point. How does this work?" He looked back to Daniel who was flipping through his book till he found what he was looking for. "Merlin? Hello?"

"Humm?" Daniel looked up at Argon. It was clear he had not heard a word they were saying and had tuned them out.

"You did not listen to a word that was said, did you?" Argon sighs and rubbed his tired eyes.

"Oh, you mean you four and Sebastian having dolls as well and us splitting up?" Okay maybe Daniel was listing. My bad. He really annoys me. I didn't even care for him when we were in school together.

"Uh, yeah… how do the dolls work?" Argon questioned again. His brow was furrowed as he watched the old wizard.

Party of me was slightly petty that he was not this old man with a long white beard and purple robes like in the old cartoons and books. He was nothing like that. He wasn't even as nice as the old man version of him. He was complete opposite. He was young and way to attractive for his own good and a bit of a cocky wanker.

"With this spell. I will need each of you to lend me your blood that will be dropped onto each doll. It will be linked to you. You will be able to watch through its eyes and guide it to do as you need. It may seem odd at first but do not worry it is not as hard as it seems. You can still do what is needed without it conflicting with what you will be doing elsewhere." Daniel explained and flipped his book around to show them. While they read the page, he made five more clay dolls and laid them out and pulled out a ritual dagger from the looks of it and quickly sliced into his own hand without hesitation or flinching at the deep cut.

"Why was that slightly attractive?" I heard Raven ask in a whisper. In response her friends giggled in agreement. I on the other hand rolled my eyes in annoyance at it.

Letting his blood drip over the doll of his choosing he began the ritual. *"Sangcruor-nus Pupa-creta."* Daniel chanted and the doll gave a glow. He looked at the other five. "Now you five will do the same and chant what I just chanted."

The five of them exchanged looks and follow his lead. Watching them each slice into their hands made me wince. The smell of blood was slightly thick in the room as each doll started to glow until they grew and took form of each of them.

We were all in amazement at the spell. It was a new one. We didn't even learn that in school. I am going to take a gander and guess we did not learn as much as his books he has kept hidden away would have to teach us.

Daniel closed his book and waved his fingers over it making it vanish from sight.

"Why was this spell never taught at school?" Chester questions while he walked around the doll version of Sebastian that still had its eyes closed.

"Many would abuse this power. That is why when I wrote the books from the spells you all use in your studies today, I left out many simply because they would be abused. This being one of them." Daniel replied to Chester and leaned on the desk in the study with his arms crossed over his chest. "Now. We need to be going. The plan Citrine laid out is good and these dolls will add as an extra aid, but they can be damaged, and they can be killed. They will turn back into the small dolls. That means be careful. Be vigilant. We do not have time to linger any longer…"

"What did you do to this woman to make her go this far?" I found myself voicing, cutting him off from talking.
Daniel's blue eyes glared at me.
"Tell us. Why… why is she doing this? What did you do Daniel… Merlin? Whatever the hell your name is… What was so bad that you are the result of so many dying?" I pressed on. I had to know. I had seen to many of my friends being killed and it all links back to this man standing before me that was so full of secrets that I could not trust him.
"Stella, drop it. We do not have time for this." Sebastian interjected. I shot him a look that I had never gave him before.
I was angry. I was so angry.
"Oh, I think we do. Does none of you question him? You just follow him blindly? He is the reason so many of our people have been killed! Him! The so-called savior. The Great Merlin." I said sarcastically. "I mean yeah… I used to believe in him. But now, now I cannot and you five. No all of you. All of you are willing to follow this man to risk dying and you don't even really know him. He is the reason for all of this. If he is our saving grace, then I think I would rather face death."
"Stella!" Sebastian looked at me in shock. All my friends did.

Daniel stood watching me. His look was dark and cold, "you are rather mouthy. If you do not want my help that is fine, but I still must do this and stop her with or without help of others. So, if you would be so kindly as to sit down and shut that pretty little mouth of yours before I do it for you."

"You will not be putting one hand on Stella." Jenna moved to her feet and placed me behind her. I looked at her surprised, "just calm down. She is right. We all do deserve an answer."

"Jenna…" I whispered and rested my forehead on her back.

"Okay. I think we all just need to breath. Just relax. We have somewhere we all need to be. So, if Daniel does tell us then it needs to be quick." James stepped forward and finally spoke up.

Daniel pinched the bridge of his nose. It was clear he was annoyed. I have a tendency to do that to people it seems. One of my many talents. "Fine. You want to know so bad then I will tell you. Thomas and Ophelia came to Camelot in June 1250. I was getting ready to go on a mission for Uther, horrible man but he was still my king, so I served him. Anyways, in passing I read both of their thoughts and what their ultimate motive was. It was one of them to either wed Morgana or Arthur and after they was wed… kill one of them. Whomever completed to goal first to gain the money and inheritance. It was mostly for Arthur. Ophelia had planned to win his heart and marry him and bore him a child to completely secure her reign as queen. Before I left, I relayed what I had gathered to Arthur. He believed me. I never got to tell Morgana, nor did Arthur. Arthur was sent out with the knights on a separate mission all on his own. I had trusted he had informed her but when I had gotten back Morgana was falling ill. I found myself working to bring her back to health, but she only kept getting sicker and I was not sure why. Ophelia kept coming to me all hours of the day wanting to be my apprentice and I wouldn't let her. I continued to turn her down, but she never let up. It got to the point where she went to the king, and he forced me to teacher her. I did not teacher her much and I kept everything important under lock and key, but it did not stop her from pushing for more from me. Not learning from me but to come to bed with me. She went as far as to find her way into my chambers and into my bed already undressed when I had come in from tending to Morgana. She wouldn't stop. But from having to entertain her I learned that she was the one poisoning Morgana. Thomas was not in on it surprisingly. While I had been away Thomas and Morgana had developed feelings for one another. It was before I confessed mine for her… Thomas was not going to go through with the plan. He had a change of heart. From reading his thoughts and his sisters it was Ophelia that was the master mind behind everything that was meant to take place… not only that."

Daniel paused and let out a heavy sigh and rubbed his eyes, "Ophelia and

Thomas, though they were siblings, they were also lovers. Ophelia was jealous of Morgana and that Thomas had feel in love with another. I wanted them both out of the kingdom, and not because I wanted Morgana for myself but because both Morgana and Arthur was in danger. Morgana was already dying, and I was doing everything I could to save her. To add to this story Morgana was to wed Thomas. Servants saw the two arguing. It was clear they had a bit of a falling out. A disagreement and I had a hunch as to what it was over. While Ophelia continued to play the part as a good and supportive Lady in Wait, I confronted Thomas one night in his chambers. I told him that I knew everything. I gave him every detail that I knew. He tried to lie his way out of it but when I told him I could read minds he froze on the spot. I told him that he had two choices. He can take his sister and leave the kingdom and I would not rat them out with evidence or I will tell the king everything even about him and his sister being lovers. It would have ruined their reputation and his sister would have been beheaded for trying to kill Morgana." He walked to the window and lent on the windowsill and watched all our expressions. "Thomas threatened to tell the Vatican what I was and have me burned at the stake but in his anger, he then took up his sword and stabbed me. I took a fall, and he went to try and finish me off, but I moved out of the way, and I took the letter opener that must have fallen on the floor when I feel and used it to stab him in the chest when he came at me again. I killed Thomas. Ophelia found out a year later and came after me for it. She had been gone from the kingdom after his death. Where she went, I did not know until she came back. I was on the out skirts of the kingdom heading out on a new quest to Argon's kingdom. She attacked me. We battled it out and then I thought I had killed her. I don't know… but it seems she is back. Happy now?" He ended the story and glared directly at me. If looks could kill I would have been dead on the spot, and he honestly could kill me with a snap of his fingers if he wanted to.

"You killed her brother and now she wants revenge?" Jenna questions.
"I would assume so." Daniel looked at his nails then back at us. "Now that story time is over, and we waisted time are we ready to go?"
I matched his glare. I still did not trust him, and I knew he was keeping things from us, but he was right on one thing, we needed to go.
"So, you murdered two possibly three royals that you swore an oath to serve and protect?" Wesley questions coldly. "And we are just supposed to believe you for the reasons you killed the other two? Argon proved the reason for

Uther but the other two how can we believe you? You wouldn't even be truthful with us from the start. The other immortals cannot read your thoughts and we are meant to just trust you. Stella has every right to not trust you. I don't. You've made it clear you would kill me. Add that to your list of royals you've murdered."

Daniel licked his lips and chuckled looking down at his oxford boots, "I do not give a damn if you both trust me or not. Right now, Clara's life is in danger along with the other students. I intend to save them. You and I can finish our banter later and I will be happy to kick your ass in front of everyone and put you in your place, I promise you that you cannot beat me. Plus, it will just be fun to show you up in front of Clara." He sighs and nods to the immortals. "Ready?" He questioned ignoring the anger that sat on Wesley's face.
"Yes, if you all will set aside your differences to get this done." Argon steps forward and held his hand up to stop us from saying anymore. "Now listen. All of you. Daniel, Sebastian, Citrine, Wesley and I will be going to the palace to deal with the problem there along with the clones of Agate and Carnelian. If anyone else want to join us say something now. If not, then you all will be going to the school."

I must admit. I was conflicted here. I did not want to leave Sebastian to go off without me given what was to come but I also want to go help aid the school. I didn't want to be that girl. The type of girl that was a love struck and based everything off emotions.
"Stella, Stevie, Chester and I will head to the school and aid them. We will form one team to handle the west entrance of the school if another group wants to form to handle the others." I looked up to see Jenna taking control on the situation. It seemed my mind was made up for me.
"Perfect. Some stay here to send to get help and be treated." Argon looked us all over and nods to someone that walked in.

"We brought in Dr. Mahoe to help us. He has been doing what he can on his end but we're getting overwhelmed with the rise in deaths and injured from all over." Luke chimes in as he brought the doctor in. "Kai, I believe you know most everyone here."
Kai gave us all a warm smile. He was a muscular built man with tan skin. His hospital was somewhere in Hawaii where he was born and raised aside from his schooling. I remembered his daughter Mililani, but we always call

he Lani. She was always so beautiful. I knew he had to be worried sick over her. "I am glad to come here and help. I wish you all good luck and be safe." With that we watched Daniel make a portal to the palace Clara was at. Him and the ones going with him vanished through it. I watched Sebastian leave to go to his sister. I prayed he would be okay. Unfortunately, I cannot say how it goes for them over there, but I can tell you how everything goes for us, and it isn't pretty.

Chapter 14

The screams from the students echoed around us when we arrived. The staff and senior students were working to keep the ward in place. I watched as Daniel's puppet acted quickly and repaired the ward and got it in place to hold. Only it did not stop the attacks on the inside that had slipped through and the ones on the outside was not letting up.

Jenna held tightly to my hand and looked down at me. "Stay by me. Do not leave my sights Stella." Her look was serious and unwavering. Part of my heart skipped a beat and I blushed. I found myself having a bit of a crush on her. Poor timing, I know and then the whole thing with Sebastian. You can judge me for that later I know I'm a hot mess. Giving her a cruet nod I let her pull me along behind her to the west side entrance.

"There is to many of them. The school is surrounded and more that got through. I do not know how long we can keep this up." Chester yelled to us as we stood back-to-back with each other fighting off the ones attacking the school. It was a mix of night walkers, warlocks, and dark witches and other things that hides in the shadows.

Stevie screamed as she watched in fear as Chester was thrown back and hit the ward. He fell to the ground in a heap. She went to run to him, but he held up his hand for her to stay back. They both looked at one another with pain. "Chester!" She screamed as a blast was sent in his direction. A rush of wind countered the spell and sent it back to the caster.

It was Agate. He appeared in front of Chester and looked down at him and held out his hand to help him up.

"Thank you." Chester winced and one of his legs buckled under him. Stevie rushed over to him. Agate eased him down and pulled up Chester's pants leg. "It's broke but I can fix it. You just have to drink my blood." Stevie looked at Agate like he was crazy when he told her what the option

was. "It will heal him quickly." Agate said to her.

Chester cupped her cheek and rested his forehead on hers. "Trust him. It will help." He said to her.

Jenna and I worked to keep the attackers at bay. I was getting tired. So much magick was being used at once and it didn't seem like it was getting any easier. They were all being fueled by this woman, and it was a never-ending supply.

"Hurry it up back there! Stella and I are getting killed out here!" Jenna yelled back to the three.

Agate cut into his hand and pressed his hand to Chester's lips. I watched in amazement at Chester's leg quickly fixing back into place and all his other injuries was healed along with his leg. "Good. You're better now get your asses up." Jenna ordered.

Chester chuckled and took Agate's hand and got to his feet with the immortals help. "Glad to see you was worried about me Jenna." He said sarcastically.

Jenna rolled her eyes and jerked me quickly back and covered me from a firry blast. She pulled up a shield over us and looked down at me. My breathing caught in my throat, and I saw her wince as part of the flames fire melted through her spell.

"J- Jenna…" I stuttered out and she only gave me a small smirk and cupped my cheek and leaned in and kissed me. I was shocked and the sounds of our friends it seemed they was as well. I leaned into the kiss more and pulled her closer and let our tongues tango together. She slowly pulled away from me and looked back at the warlock that was closing in on us.

"Stay put. I'm not done with you." She whispered to me and moved herself off me leaving me to gather my thoughts on what just happened with what she had just said. I went to open my mouth, but nothing came out but a little squeak. My eyes were locked on her as I sat up and watched her raise her hand. "Ignis-Grando." She called out and a swirl of fire and ice seemed to swarm around the male incasing him in the flames of both causing him to scream out in pain until he combusted in front of us. My mouth dropped open in shock and I looked back at her and watched her eyes on me. She had a smirk on her face, and she looked me over. "Are you okay little thing?" She questioned me and helped me to my feet. "You're blushing." She stated.

"I- um… you… what?" I squeaked out and felt my face get even more red and her being as close as she was to me was not helping the situation.

"So… as adorable as this is between you two… we need to keep fighting." Chester chuckled and nods for us to follow him and the others.

"Try not to die little thing. I want to have a chance with you." Jenna teased me and took my arm and pulled me to follow.

Really, what just happened? I am still trying to process this but there is way too much going on for me to even comprehend it. But what was about to happen next, I did not expect.

"Allow me to make this easy on all of you. Hand over the one you all call Daniel Smith Jr and I will be so kind as to spare you lives for the time being." A voice echoed out to us all. "We know Merlin is one of your classmates and we know he goes by Daniel. Hand him over and your lives will be spared."

"That must be Ophelia." Agate looked up to the sky where the voice was coming from. "We need to hurry and take out what we can. I do not trust that we won't see worse even if the students turn on Merlin."

"Surely they would not do that." I replied but judging by Jenna and Chester's face I was about to be proven wrong.

"They did last year." Agate said back to me. Shock washed over mine and Stevie's faces.

I couldn't believe it. Then again Daniel was not liked by many at the school between students and staff. He was intelligent and he did not hesitate to correct someone and let them know they was wrong. It was more of the male population though. The girls fawned over him, but he always seemed to ignore them.

"I will give you all thirty minutes to turn him over to me or this school and everyone in it will be no more." Ophelia's voice echoed out over the school. Panic sat in over the students on what to do but it did not take long for plenty to speak up read to throw Daniel to the wolves.

""Our revels now ended. These our actors,
As I foretold you, were all spirits and
Are melted into air, into thin air:
And, like the baseless fabric of this vision,
The cloud-capp'd towers, the gorgeous places,
The solemn temples, the great globe itself,

Yea, all which it inheart, shall dissolve
And, like this insubstantial pageant faded,
Leave not a rack behind. We are such stuff
As dreams are made on, and our little life
Is rounded with a sleep.'"
-The Tempest, Act 4, Scene 1 by William Shakespeare. Fine. She wants me.
She can have me." I heard his voice and as much as I hated him my heart
dropped at his words.

"Merlin. You cannot do this. That would be suicide!" Agate argued.

"One life is not more important that billions of lives on this planet. Her and
I have some unfinished business. My puppet self is still here and able to aid.
I will try and defuse the situation quickly and trap her away…" Daniel was
cut off from replying to Agate when we heard a voice calling out to him.

"Merlin!" The voice yelled out. It was Romeo. He quickly pulled Daniel
into his arms and hugged him. Tears ran down his face and he cried into
Daniel's neck. "You're alive… y- you're alive."

Daniel frowns and hugged Romeo back. "I am sorry old friend to have
worried you, but I need to go. I have unfinished business with Ophelia."

"What? No, I will not allow this… you cannot!" Romeo pulled away and
wipes his tears away and glared at Daniel with sad angry eyes.

"I'll go with him." I chime in and quickly covered my mouth, and everyone
looked at me shocked.

"Absolutely not!" Jenna protested. "You both are asking for trouble."

"Jenna, we are all already in deep shit. We're trying to fight this thing from
the outside when we need to be on the inside. We cannot win it this way.
Just look at everything around us." I motioned at the destruction all around
us.

"Fine, then I am coming as well." Jenna said to me after a long while.

"We all will. You're not going at it alone." Agate chimes in.

"Hell no. You could all end up dead. We have no clue what we are
walking into right now." Daniel said to us. "I am not letting it happen."

"You need the help, Merlin. You thought you killed this woman, but you
didn't and now we have no clue what to expect. She very well may have a
way to end your life for good." Agate replied calmly. "Do not be a fool. Let
us help you."

Weighing his options, he finally said something, "okay, fine. Let us see what
will happen." Turning his attention up to the heavens we hear him call out,

"Ophelia! You want me? Well, here I am! Leave everyone else alone!"
Almost like static coming through I watch in shock as she started to make
Daniel vanish. I quickly grab on to him and the last thing I heard was our
friends screaming for us.

Landing hard on a cold ground I tried to let my eyes adjust to everything
around me. I felt Daniel hold me close to him, his breathing was shaky, and
his heart was pounding in his chest. Part of me started to feel guilty so not
trusting him. "Daniel… where are we?" I asked in a whisper.

"You are in Purgatory my dears. I went fishing for an old wizard and got
another catch. In the process. Lucky me. A new toy to play with." A voice
sounded out from the darkness. I knew it was Ophelia. It was the same
voice from earlier. I just couldn't see her and the necklace around my skin
was on fire and cracked, crumbling to the ground.

"Show yourself Ophelia!" Daniel shouted into the darkness.

"Oh, do not get so grumpy my dear Merlin. I only wanted you. Not her but I
will make do with this." The sounds of heels echoing in the darkness
sounded around us until a woman appeared and the mist moved away that
had coated us. She was beautiful. Long ink back hair, she had this body that
was too perfect to be real and perfect pale skin. She was gorgeous. She knelt
in front of us and tilted Daniel's chin up to meet her black eyes. "Oh, how I
have missed that look of hate from those perfect blue eyes. Still just as
handsome as the day we first met." She glanced at me, and I took in a sharp
breath and hid more in Daniel's arms. The scent of Mont Blanc lingered on
his suit that he wore and the Amethyst he wore around his neck caught my
eyes it matched the one Clara always wore. "Now to separate you both."
Daniel jerked away from her, and she yanked him back to her. Her eyes
dropped to his necklace, and she smirked yanking it off him tossing it away
like it was trash. The color drained from his face as he watched the little
crystal hit the floor and slide away. She shook him back to get his attention
as she pulled me from his embrace and tossed me aside and I found myself
behind bars that was not there before.

"Stop! Let him go!" I screamed out but she ignored me. "Daniel! Do
something!"

"Oh, my dear he cannot. His powers are no good here. You see I am not
dead nor living. I am what all darkness and nightmares are made of. I
ensured my fate when I made sure Merlin killed me. It was not easy, but I
gained my powers with each sacrifice. Areses helped guide me with that.
You taking him from me made it harder. I did complete it though. Each

abandoned village I made vanish. All those odd untold stories of what happened to these places was my doing to give me the darkness that I now hold and you killing me helped complete it to make this. Now I can make mankind suffer and bend at my will. Soon I will be able to bring Areses and Thomas back. Both you selfishly took from me."

Daniel swallowed hard and I could tell he was trying to will his powers to work just like I was but nothing. Nothing happened. I felt helpless and I could see he did as well. "Send her back... she does not have to be here." He finally said and dropped his hands down beside his side and stopped fighting.

"Don't you dare give up Daniel! Fight her!" I screamed. I couldn't believe what I was seeing. He was ready to give up simply because his powers were not working in this place.

"Will you shut up girly?" Ophelia got to her feet and three-night walkers came out and my eyes went wide. "Oh, you know them, do you?" "M- Mark... how... how could you?" My eyes burned with tears. Mark looked away from me. He held hurt in his eyes as he jerked Daniel up with Jay's help and took him to be chained up. "Don't do this... Please Mark!" I pleaded but again he said nothing to me as he clasped the chains to Daniel's wrists and one around his neck. Tears rolled down my face. Someone I trusted had turned on us or had been working against us the whole time. "I will figure out how to stop you Ophelia... just you wait." I heard Daniel finally say as Jay force Daniel to his knees.

"I would not count on it my dear Merlin. I will be draining your powers for the final part of this spell that will bring back both my lovers. You will die and everything you trapped away will be freed once and for all and then I can shroud all in darkness." Ophelia walked over to him slowly as he glared at her. "Now this will hurt, and you will suffer, and I will enjoy hearing you scream in pain." She smirked and eyed his hand. "Ah, and before you summon that dragon of yours..." She removed his ring that had two dragons circling two Amethyst gem like eggs in a way like they were guarding them. Then it hit me. The two gems on the ring symbolized Morgana and Merlin and how his dragon always protected them and still does.

I watched the ring hit the ground and slide away. Daniel looked pale. Ophelia held up her hand and there it was. This black crystal ball looking thing in hand. Moving her hands, it floated and gave off this dark red eerie glow. Then it happened. The light erupted from it and hit Daniel. I watched on in horror. Gripping the bars, I screamed. I screamed his name and tears stained my face. "DANIEL!"

I watched him struggle and pull at his bindings to get free but to no aval. He held back his own screams. I could tell he was in pain and that the thing was killing him.

"Stop it! Stop! Mark Please help! Don't Do this!" I screamed and sobbed shaking and pulling at the bars on my prison where I was forced to watch this play out.

Ophelia chuckled darkly as she watched Daniel struggle to break free. "Struggle all you want Merlin. You will not get free."

I drop to my knees and sob heavily. "Mark... Please!"

Mark looked at me sadly and mouthed *'sorry'* to me. I could tell he did not want to do it, but I did not understand why he did. Was he that scared of this woman? Then again just seeing and being part of all of this and watching her even overpower Merlin... I was scared also. I was trying to think I had to do something. I could not be the useless girl in this story that needed saving even thought I was right now. My eyes landed on Daniel's ring and then it clicked. *'His ring.'* I thought to myself. *'The dragon.'*

Chapter 15

Daniel was still struggling to not let Ophelia win out, but I could tell he was getting weaker. He did not look at me, but I heard him in my thoughts.

'I heard you. Some magick must work here for her to do away with both my necklace and ring. Get my ring. Call on Amethyst.' I heard him say to me. The pain in his voice broke my heart. I felt like such a bitch for how I was earlier to him.

Watching what was happening I look back at Mark who avoided my eyes. Everyone seemed busy so I took my chance and I reached for the ring. I was coming up short. I kept stretching digging my nails into the ground and pushing myself against the bars to try and reach it. It hurt. I couldn't lie about that. Seeing two shoes in front of me but facing away I looked up to see the back of Mark. He took his heels and moved the ring closer to me and I grabbed it. I let out a shaky breath and looked at him again. He still did not look my way. I knew he was ashamed.

'I have it.' I reached my mind out to Daniel the best I could. Looking at the beautiful ring he always wore I ran my fingers over it and the gems on it glowed purple. Then I heard it. His scream. I snapped my head up to see Daniel screaming out in pain as the light from him was pulled out of him only leaving what looked like a crystal floating above him and then his body collapsing to the ground. "No! Amethyst!" I screamed. The ring lit up in a bright light that made the bars on the prison bust away and this large dragon screeched to life. The anger behind the dragon showed.

Ophelia turned around quickly to be face to face with the purple dragon who held anger in his large emeralds. I darted quickly from where I was at and snatched up the necklace, "grab her!" She screamed and the dragon knocked back Jay and Skyler with his tail. They hit the wall hard and fall to the ground. Mark hesitated and Ophelia caught on and sent a black blast to Mark but he moved quickly out of the way and rushed over to Daniel and took a knee next to me to help undo the shackles on the wizard. "You idiot!" She yelled at Mark.

"I am sorry Miss. Stella. I never wanted this to happen... she was going to kill all the others like me if I didn't... please forgive me." Mark said and held the glowing life crystal from Daniel. "I do not know what to do to fix this." He gave it to me to figure out.

Amethyst breathed out a blast of purple flames and Ophelia blocked. She eyed Mark and me and sent off another spell that I didn't know with each being black when casted. Mark quickly moved in front to block me and took the hit. I screamed and watched him drop to his knees. My mind was racing. I did not know what to do. I looked at the still floating ball. Then to what was in my hand.

"Amethyst! The black ball! Blow on it or something! Break it! It might undo what was done to Merlin..." I yell out. I slip his ring back on his hand and placed his necklace in his hand. I look back at Mark and take him in my arms. "Mark... please don't die... I forgive you..."

He chuckled sadly. "You are so kind and beautiful Stella... Sebastian is a lucky man." He cupped my cheek and tears rolled down my face as I kissed the palm of his hand and watched the light start to fade from his eyes.

"Mark... Mark!" I screamed and his body went limp, and his hand dropped to the side. Tears burnt as they slid down my face. I screamed and cried into his chest. Mark was gone. He was really gone. It felt like time had stopped and everything started to move in slow motion.

The sound of something exploding pulled me out of Mark's chest. Shards of the black ball rained down over us, and I watched as Ophelia hit the dragon hard causing it to fly back and bust through a wall in this prison called Purgatory. A loud whimper from the dragon and it landed in a loud heap on the floor and went back to being a small size. His head lifted and it never took its eyes off Daniel. It seemed to try and force itself up and to grow again to be able to go by his master's side and protect him. "Amethyst go back in the ring you cannot keep fighting. You did good." I said to him and got to my feet.

Hearing a wicked laugh, I watched as she hit Amethyst again and the dragon screeched out in pain. "Stop it!" I yelled. I did not know what else I could do. Daniel was still dead. At least I think he is. The crystal that had come

out of him was still not back in him. Mark was dead from saving my life and Jay and Skyler was unconscious. I was the last one standing, and my odds did not look promising.

"Or what? You have no power here. I will admit you surprised me by bringing out this pesky dragon of Merlin's. His loyal little companion. You even managed to destroy the crystal ball, but you have still lost. I finally won against Merlin." Ophelia walked over to Amethyst and yanked him up by the nap of his neck and threw him across the room making him land hard next to Daniel. He yelped and cried out but still forced himself to move closer to Daniel. I watched in shock. Amethyst rested his head on Daniel's chest and tears ran down his face out of pain and sadness. "Now it is your turn." I snap my head around to look at her. I was an open target, and I was at a loss on what to do. I was a dead woman standing.

"No... that being destroyed should have reversed the spell.... It had to of." I said in disbelief. "I was sure it would work..."
"Were you now? Well, it seems you got it wrong." Ophelia walked slowly over to me.
I had to do something. I had to bring Daniel back. He can end her. He figured out what to do but he was too late to stop her. There must be a way to restore him.
Then it clicked.
I knew what I had to do.
Dropping to my knees next to him I took the life of the crystal and held it over him. "Amethyst... Please try to hold her off. I know you are tried and hurt but I think I can bring back Daniel. Can you help me?"
He lifted his head and nods to me and forced his weak legs to hold him up. I felt horrible for asking him to do it, but I needed to buy time. I watched him force himself to grow again and blow flames from his largemouth again keeping her at bay. It kept being a game of block and attack repeatedly between the two.
"Okay Daniel... let's get you back..." I whispered and closed my eyes. I channeled his life force from the crystal that came out of him and the ones he wore to tap into my own. It hurt but I did not stop. We needed him. I had made a mistake in not trusting him. Who knows maybe we still can't but given what we're up against he really is the lesser of the evils at hand? My head started to spin as I watched the crystal slowly sink back into him and I smiled weakly as I watched his eyes slowly open showing his curillin blues.

"Welcome back Merlin…" I whispered and gripped at the floor before I collapsed.

Daniel sat up quickly and looked at me with wide eyes. "What did you… you didn't… Stella!"

"Damn you!" Ophelia screamed in anger.

"It had to be done. Go save everyone. Stop her Daniel… Just tell everyone… tell them I love them…" I said to him and cupped his cheek. "I am sorry for how I treated you." My eyes closed and I was gone. This is how I died. I died saving Merlin. Our hero in this story. In this crazy chaotic story that I have tried to do my best at telling you. This might be the end for me, but it isn't for the others and most defiantly not for Merlin.

Chapter 16

"Stella... Stella!" I yelled and shook her lifeless body, "damn you Ophelia... Damn you! Why still hold this grudge? Why attack and kill everyone else when I am your problem? They're not involved!" I yelled at her. Getting to my feet I clinched my necklace in my hand and felt the energy radiate off it and send a rush of power threw me along with my blood running over it from my nails digging painfully into my palm. I knew what I had to do. "Amethyst! Retreat. You have done well old friend. Take a break." Calling back Amethyst, he went back into my ring where he resides and builds back up his energy and power.

"Oh, lucky me. I get the ever so great Merlin all to myself. What now Merlin? You have no power here. I do. You are on my playing field. That girl was a fool to exchange her life to bring back yours. Clever trick though." Ophelia laughed that same laugh that I always hated. It was demonic and sent chills down my spine. "At least Delemer will be happy to know that you are alive."
I froze.
"What?" That name always made my skin crawl. His obsession with me never seemed to end. I felt sick at the sound of that ice demons name. "I sealed him away. There is no way he is free."
"Oh? You just died. Do you not think that a few of them did not escape?" She replied to me with a sweet innocent smile that held venom behind it.
I had no response. She was right. It was very likely and that only meant more trouble for us all and I had yet to deal with this one. I was not prepared for any of this. My own pride had blinded me and now it was leading many to death. I am such a fool. I know better than to let my pride blind me, but I did just that.
"Merlin at a loss for word? Now that is a shock. You have always been so

good at running that mouth of yours. Seems now there is something that can shut you up." Ophelia walked closer to me until she was standing in front of me running her hands up my chest and let one of her hands wrap around my tie, I flinched away only for her to jerk my tie pulling me back to her. "Such a shame. We could have been so much more Merlin, but you had to go and pick Morgana over me." She whispered up at me.

"You are nothing but pure evil. We would have never been anything regardless of Morgana." I replied to her and tapped into my necklace and started to chant in my head the spell repeatedly to seal her away.

Ophelia furrowed her brow and clung to me as she started to weaken. "What is going on? What is happening to me?" She looked at her hands then back up at me and saw the Amethyst in my palm glowing. Damn you Merlin!" She screamed and held up her hand and blasted me back with a spell.

Hitting the ground, I looked up and the cloudy sky outside the school. I coughed out a breath and rolled over gathering myself before I sat up. The school grounds were a mess. I have no clue what happened while we were trapped in Purgatory, but it seems like they all put up one hell of a fight. Glancing over I found Mark and Stella's bodies. The other two was missing. Crawling over to the young redheaded girl I gently brushed her hair from her face and looked her over sadly.

"Merlin!" I snap my head around to see Argon rushing over to me. "What the hell happened? You've been gone for days."

'Days?' I said to myself, "how is that possible? What day is it?"

"October 30. You've all been gone a week… What happened to Stella and Mark?" Argon asked me.

"Stella!" We look over to see Sebastian and the others running over to us. He froze as he looked down at Stella's body that was on the ground unmoving. "Stella…." He struggled to get her name out. "What happened to her?"

How could I tell him that she died by giving me her life?

"What happened to them?" Chester looked over their bodies and held Stevie in her arms who let out a pained scream as she sobbed. Jenna was trying to hold it together, but she was on the verge of tears as well.

"You were meant to protect her! Save her and us all! You're Merlin! We trusted you! I trusted you!" Sebastian shouted at me and jerked me up by my collar. My chest felt tight. It was hard keeping eye contact. I did fail

them. I had no idea what I was walking into, and I let my ego and pride get in the way and it costed the lives of others as a result. He shoved me back and I stumbled. The sudden feel of isolation hit me. The feel of losing comrades was weighing on me. Words from the past rushing back to me. *'They will all turn on you in the end. You will be alone at the end of this Merlin.'*

"It was my fault. Our powers were useless in this things Ophelia calls Purgatory. Stella died trying to save us. Save me… Ophelia had killed me… she found a way… Stella found a way to bring me back and that was by exchanging her life for mine. Where she learned that spell… she must have looked at your books Sebastian the ones that Argon gave you… I am truly sorry Sebastian… all of you." I said to them. "I promise I will stop Ophelia. Now I know exactly what we are dealing with, but we have more trouble to deal with. I will do everything to stop it all… I will not let her death be in vain."

Sebastian half laughed and shook his head, "tell that to her parents. I am done with you and helping you. She was right to not trust you. So was Wesley." Was Sebastian's last words to me before he stormed off.

"I am sorry…" I whispered and lowered my head in shame and wrapped my arms around me. They left me to stand there alone as they took both the bodies away.

October 30, 2021

"For ever and for ever farewell, Brutus. If we do meet again, we'll smile; indeed, if not, 'tis true this parting was well made." With a heavy heart I quoted William Shakespeare's Julius Caesar, Act 5 Scene 1. I rested my forehead on the tape recorder in my hand before going on. *'I could have brought her back. Used up one of my lives, but I didn't. I was to drained. There is more to this thing Ophelia calls Purgatory than I thought. We did not just lose hours, we lost days. Being stuck in it drains the life out of you slowly even without the crystal she used on me to pull out my own life crystal. She is death and darkness. I am going to have to be careful. One wrong move and…'* I sigh.

"This is Stella's final journal entry. I am truly sorry Stella. I promise you. I will avenge you and everyone who has fallen because of me.
Sincerely,
Merlin."

Appendix

Spells

- Healing Spell- Sancrumed
- Sealing Away Spell- Cione Auferetur Quodperiit Malum Unus
- Protection Spell- Praturpro
- Stun Spell- Obstupefacio
- Cursed Dagger 1 Pain- Passioadflic
- Cursed Dagger 2 Sleep- Sompor
- Revers/Undo Spell- Abrogo Novis
- Breakthrough Shield/Barrier Spell- Esperanto Rompi
- Only Darkness Spell- Nisi Tebebrae
- Unable to Breath Spell- Nec de Resp
- Purify Spell- Liquet de Proluo
- Blood Puppet- Sangcruo-nus Pupa-creta
- Fire Ice Flames Spell- Ignis-Grando

Darkness Unfolds:
The Return of Merlin

Chapter 1

The moon hung high in the night sky with stars that dusted the navy blue to black that coated the evening. Pulling my motorbike to a stop next to a sidewalk to take a break I pulled my helmet off to shake out my hair before running my fingers through it. I was only planning on passing through to get to my next destination and my bike needed gas. From this stop I got an odd feeling that this town was not normal. Something was off about it. Furrowing my brows together I looked up and down the almost deserted road in the town. Catching my eye across the street I spotted a diner that held a vintage style to it. Dismounting the bike, I grabbed my rucksack and threw it over my shoulders and grabbed the other bag to make my way across the street. I had my leather jacket zipped up as the evening air cut through me and even in that chill, I could feel something was not quite right with the town I had stopped in.

Opening the doors to the diner I slipped in hearing the bells give a ring. I let my eyes wonder over the interior of the place that looked like something out of a 50's television show, like time has stood still. Removing my rucksack, I sat it in the booth I chose to sit in. Taking notice, it was not a busy night but then again, I was coming through rather late. Taking the menu that was on the table I read through what was listed. A slight scowl crossed my supple lips and let out a sigh and rolled my eyes. I was starting to grow tired of quick foods. I had been on the road for far too long and it was wearing on me. Playing with my ring that had two dragons in circling two amethyst crystals I let my mind start to wonder. Rubbing my tired eyes, I rested

my elbows on the table. I was going to hope they had hot teas. I was not one for coffee, but it seemed rather unlikely. Then there was the problem of finding a place to bunk for the night before hitting the road the next morning to get out of town.

"You're not out of the woods yet Daniel." I said to himself. At least that was the name I was going by now. The less people knew about me the better and the less people I got attach to the better. At least that is what I tell myself.

Rubbing my hand on my face I sighs heavily and looked back at the menu then pushed it away and waited for someone to serve me but out of habit I kept messing with my ring or necklace. It was a nervous habit of mine. Keeping the same tired but serious gaze I let my eyes take in the building and studying the people in it. I could feel magick in the air. And no not the romantic kind. It was a mix of dark and light and it seemed as if both was fighting to outweigh the other.
"I really do need to get out of this town." I whispered to myself.
"Wouldn't you agree Amethyst?" A little snout pokes out of my rucksack, and I pressed my index finger to my lip as if to hush the little purple dragon that looked up at me with big green eyes. Smiling down at my companion I chuckled softly. "I'll get you food boy but for now you have to stay hidden. If anything, I'll get it To-Go so we can go find a room and I can feed you…. Now do not give me that look." I scowl as I talked in hushed tones to Amethyst. It was always like this with the two of us. Amethyst could grow in size and would normally be in my ring resting but he insisted on riding with me out of the ring where he resided. "You would think after almost three centuries you would be nicer to me." I grumbled and gave Amethyst a side glance and was only greeted with a smile. Shaking my head, I poked Amethyst back into my rucksack before he was seen.

"Sorry about your wait sweetheart. What can I get for you tonight?" A young woman asked and seemed to take a keen interest in me, or

so it seemed, "you're not from around here, are you?" She questioned.

I pierced my lips together and raised a brow. "No. I am not." I gave a short reply without giving her much of a look.

A slight pout rested on her lips at my ability to ignore her looks.

"I'd like to place my order To-Go if you will. I'll have one cheeseburger with the side of chips... fries. Sorry you lot call them fries here.... And I'll also take your grilled shrimp skewers and a side salad. No dressing. Oh, and a hot cup of black tea. I will need the milk for it on the side." I instructed.
"Defiantly not from around here." She jotted everything down taking note of my accent and that seemed to only make her more interested. "I- I will get this right out for you. Would you like a cup of tea while you wait for you food to be prepped to take home?"

I frowned at the words *"home,"* licking my lips I gave her a half smile. "That would be lovely. Thank you." She nods to me and leaves me alone to go turn in my order.

Home.

A word I was not familiar with. *'At least not since... yes... then.'* I said to himself in my mind set. The clanking of a cup and saucer was sat in front of me with a side of milk. Looking up at the young woman that gave me a worried look that I only returned with a polite smile and nod, "thank you ma'am."

"Are you okay?" She asked me.
"Yes, no need to fret. Thank you for your concern." I replied to her, "where is your closest place for lodging for the night," I inquired.

"Oh. Here. Just up those stairs are the rooms you can rent from the owner of this diner. I can help get you sat up. How many nights will you be staying?" She perked up as she watched me.

I went about adding the white sugar first with only a teaspoon and then adding the milk after, "only for tonight." I stirred in the mix without looking back at her. Just by the sound of a slight disappointment leaving her lips from the sigh she took let me know what her facial expression was.

"Hopefully you'll change your mind by morning, but I will go talk to the owner and get you a room key. I can show you up after your food comes out." The waitress looked back down at me with sad eyes before walking away with a pout.

I leaned back more on the booth set and closed my eyes for a moment to think. The warmth on from the teacup I had my hands wrapped around warmed me up slightly. *"365 days. That is how long I have been..."* I did not finish my thought. It pained me too much to do that. My chest tightened and a flash of her face crossed my memory. No matter how hard I wanted to forget her. I couldn't. Her laughter echoed in my mind with flashes of her blue eyes that seemed to smile at me. *"God how I missed her."* Reluctantly I brought the hot liquid to my lips and took a sip of it. It wasn't as good as what they had back in Europe, but it was to be expected. I had been in the states long enough to know that and lived many lives to learn it as well. It would never measure up to a proper English tea or what they had in Italy at least.

Made in the USA
Columbia, SC
13 March 2023

13592205R00065